NESSIM
A CODA

NESSIM
A CODA

Frank Kersnowski

ORANGE *frazer* PRESS
Wilmington, Ohio

ISBN 978-1949248-654

Published for the copyright holder by:
Orange Frazer Press
37½ West Main St.
P.O. Box 214
Wilmington, OH 45177

For price and shipping information, call: 937.382.3196
Or visit: www.orangefrazer.com

Book and Cover design:
Orange Frazer Press with Catie South

Library of Congress Control Number: 2022916125

First Printing

This book is dedicated to my friend Lucia Graves and my mentor Lawrence Durrell.

Together four novels constitute 'The Alexandria Quartet:' a suitable descriptive subtitle would be 'a word continuum.' (*Clea* p. 7)

Acknowledgments of those who have read and encouraged me to continue writing: David Edwards, Lucia Graves, Richard Pine, and John Presley.

TABLE OF CONTENTS

PREFACE

In 1935 Lawrence Durrell and his wife Nancy moved from England to Corfu, preceding his widowed mother and his three siblings. There they lived as expats with money in a society only modestly informed about money. Gerald Durrell in *The Corfu Trilogy* and his brother Lawrence in *Prospero's Cell* have described their idyllic life. Not surprisingly, their peasants are remarkably similar: getting up before dawn and working past dusk, living by the phases of the moon and the demands of the seasons, knowing little of banks and nothing of the people who ran them. For the Wordsworths and the Durrells the peasants were a happy people who loved the land and loved their work, a people who deserved the literary celebrations of their lives. From one group came oral literature and from the other the printed word.

Such was the idyllic world the Durrells inhabited happily until the anticipated arrival of the German army caused Mother Durrell and three of her children (Leslie, Margo, and Gerry) to return to what Larry called Pudding Island, a moribund England—stolid and humorless. Larry, Nancy, and daughter Penelope (aka Ping Ku) moved steadily south, finally settling in Alexandria, Egypt in 1942. There the marriage dissolved. Later Nancy snorted in derision when she was told Larry said the break up was a casualty of war. What Larry described to Henry Miller as "literally being up to my ears" in the sexual provender of Alexandria may have played a role in the break up.

In Alexandria, Durrell began talking, again of the long incubating *The Book of the Dead.* There it found a nurturing, if unwanted, nest, a culture sufficiently corrupt and complex to foster the moral deformities for which he himself was not immune. Durrell, like most of the other English, especially those who had lived in the same Greece he had, hated the flat, arid Egypt, which they regarded as venal and shallow. They eschewed any concern for the role of the British Colonial impulse in creating modern Egypt.

While living in Cyprus and then in the south of France from 1956 to 1960, Durrell would revisit his war years in Egypt, and would recall and recast that time with its "sexual provender," largely prewar, in four volumes that used the life of a Coptic Egyptian family, the Hosanis. They were angered by the insolent rejection of the Copts during the British Protectorate of Egypt and the British Mandate of Palestine and justifiably frightened by a Muslim dominance they were certain would occur when the Protectorate and the Mandate ended (ostensibly) in 1947. Writing when he did, Durrell had the benefit of hindsight. The Coptic community was and so continues to be discriminated against and violated since Moslem Egypt came into power. The Copts are the majority of those receiving exit visas, and their population continues to decline. And the culture of the Egypt that he portrayed continues to provide evidence of the moral and immoral propensities of our species. All occurs in an exotic setting, a narrative that, as he told me, was "contemporary." Though I did not ask, I assumed based on his writings after that to be contemporary was to acknowledge the societal and personal identities that struggled to exist in a world of political and personal compromise.

His choice of Egypt before, during, and after World War II makes sense. The absence of a traditional morality during the War and the implacable movement away from the political identities of the past provided a setting for his study: human beings deprived of past social and cultural norms and a society caught between the politics of the past and the emerging power of the future. And his decision to focus his narrative on the struggle of the Copts to protect their role in Egypt by allying themselves with Jewish fighters in Palestine makes good fictional, in not historic, sense.

Durrell's *Quartet* ties all loves and lusts to this plot and created a burst of fictive life in the morgue of the literary sixties. The setting is exotic, neither drab middle class America nor the bareness of working class England. Comparison with the later caused Durrell to refer to himself as "an angry old Camembert." Even in faraway Egypt, all characters are comprehensible. All affairs and erotic misalliances are comprehensible. Everything makes good fictive sense. Except for the central motivations. Why would a Coptic family, wealthy in land

and financial holdings, risk all? And why would Nessim, the spoiled priest son of a secular family, become so passionately committed to the plot? And why would he marry without desire the divorced Jew Justine, that sexual turnstile through whom they all passed, to quote Durrell's creation the British writer and embassy employee Pursewarden? Surely, other Jewish women could have provided his bona fides to the Jewish fighters to whom he would provide guns in exchange for protection in the new Egypt. We know that Nessim has an affair with Melissa who was the lover of another Embassy employee, Darley, and that she dies giving birth to their daughter. We know little of what happens after this. Just that the child and Darley live together on a remote Greek island and, in time Darley takes the child to Alexandria where she is united with her father and the Dark Queen, Justine.

Reflecting on these questions and issues, I have come to see *The Quartet* as one of those iconic works that troubles ones sleep because they burrow into the very matrix, physical, intellectual, and emotional, of who we are. They invite the readers to place themselves into such a world, to inhabit it, and wonder what they would have done. And these works invite the writer to recast the narratives, or parts, into different times and places, as James Joyce did with *The Odyssey*: the chaste Penelope becomes the wayward wife Molly Bloom. The concurrence of this duality exemplifies what Stith Thompson called "the tested wife motif." Fortunately for Odysseus and Leopold Bloom no "tested husband motif" exists. That far lesser writers than Joyce have cast *The Odyssey* into other times and the characters into other fictional beings has emboldened me to extend Durrell's iconic work and hopefully not diminish it by recasting parts of *The Quartet*, positing some back stories, and saying "what if this had been the case."

In what follows I take liberties with *The Quartet,* especially *Mountolive,* and in my readings of Durrell's later works, especially *The Avignon Quintet.* I have somewhat added to the form of the Hosnani family's desert home, Karm Abu Girg, by making it a bit shabbier than it seems in *The Quartet.* My reason for doing so is based on what George Weidenfelt wrote in *Remembering My Good Friends*, his autobiography: that he had visited the desert homes of Jews he thought were the models for Hosnani's residence. The other major change I made is my portrayal of Leila, the mother of Nessim and Narouz and wife of Falhus. In Durrell's telling she is disappointed that she was forced to return from Europe, where she thrived, and forced into an arranged marriage with a much older man. She retained in her room books, journals, art works, and vestiges of her lost world. But in my view she did much more than that. She became the intellectual force behind the Coptic plot. She not only had the intelligence, she had, in my view, contacts with the Jewish community. And she had the creative urge strengthened by a, then, celibate and loveless marriage. Her relationship with her son Nessim I construct from asides in *Mountolive* and from my reflections on Durrell's interest in Freud and Jung.

Other liberties I have taken are found in characters I have created, some derived from Durrell and some from my own suppositions. Those who are interested in these endeavors will easily find most answers in *Mountolive*. However, two of my creations come not from *The Quartet*. The narrator of three volumes of *The Quar-*

tet is a seedy Irish academic named Darley. I have replaced him with Charles Robertson, an American who goes as the wind blows him and does what he can to survive. I have not granted him the role of narrator, though in all other respects he is a close semblance to Darley. Also a bit seedy, he is a wanderer who was easily seduced by Justine. For he is a willing subject of strong women. The actual narrator is unnamed, as was the narrator of *Mountolive,* though like Charles he is from Appalachia. And then borrowing narrative ploys from *The Quintet*, I have taken characters from their home volumes and placed them anew. I have also allowed them to become acquainted with their author. To do this, I have made Durrell himself a character in *Nessim.* My intent here is to posit a what if this iconic work with its troubling characters were cast in a place and time that bears scant familiarity to Durrell's.

Hopefully what I have written will remind all of us, if such is needed, of the world shaking effect of *The Quartet* when it first appeared and shook the sixties out of its literary doldrums. It is not *South Wind* capturing us by exotica. It is *Lord Jim*, freeing characters from the readers' everyday life the better to allow the writer to delve into essential humanity.

In so doing, I have had the benefit of comments and commentaries and by talks with Durrell. I can but hope, not vainly perhaps, that Durrell would respond to what I have done with his masterpiece as he did when I talked with him about the narrative structure of *Tunc* and *Nunquam*. "Well, is that what you did?" To which he replied: "No. But I like it."

NESSIM

A CODA

CHAPTER ONE

With bowed heads and still whispering prayers to St. Bishoy, the pilgrims left Wadi el Natrun. The sun was setting over the sacred oasis which housed the bodies of the Coptic saints and attendant monks as the nine pilgrims went back to Alexandria. That morning they had gathered in front of the Cecil, a hotel none of them could afford. Ten left on their pilgrimage. Only nine returned. The tenth, a slender man with dark hair and beard wore his hat tilted over the left eye. Usually he wore an eye patch to cover the eye that looked on nothing. One more observant than the pilgrims would have noticed that his clothes though worn were not cheap and tattered as were theirs. His blue suit and black shoes though old were bespoke, as the careful hand stitching on the cap of the shoes and the lapels of the coat showed. In a better time, he had gone to Jermyn Street for his shoes and Savile Row for his suits after lunch at his club. For now, though, the world of London clubs and bespoke shoes and suits was past. Yet called from memory by labels bearing the century old names of craftsmen was the smell of leather and the quiet bustle of clerks. Soon, all this, too, would be lost, with his memories, lost in a room where for centuries monks had left their memories. In a time better than Nessim's, on the other side of the Med, I had myself been housed in a monastery. I had gone to escape the tension of marriage and the cries of a child to be with Greek monks in a silence marked only by the sound of monks farting in their cells, "love calls of old Byzantium" as my friend Larry once observed. Nessim's stay had more urgency, more quiet. For only his mind sounded and echoed with the trials of the past, the nervous possibility of the future.

The small bus with the peeling camouflage paint had almost as bad a war as the passengers it picked up at seven that morning. The refugees in the remnants of clothes gathered from work camps and tenements stood silently with eyes averted from one another. They boarded the bus and sat separately not speaking, not looking out the windows as the bus traveled toward the Great Western Desert on the EI Alamein Road. El Alamein an obscure railroad station is dyed forever in memory by the battle over 1500 miles and the thousands who died in it. Those on the bus were not to see the ruins of war machinery. They were not to see the graves that later would be marked by memorials. An English garden, a bougainvillea draped fence, a sandstone and marble monolith. Their silence was as intense as that of the desert which retained the now inwardly resonant sounds of war. Gone but not forgotten as the cliché has it. It would never be forgotten, not in the desert and not in the ruined faces and bodies that endured and made survival a term best used in newsreels to be seen by people who had no experiences of such death and fear. Of course, present was the one exception who in manner only seemed not unlike his fellows. But he alone had had a better war, a worse peace.

Standing, face averted, Nessim strove for and achieved anonymity, though not forgetfulness, so he mused: "For me the war was a respite, to use a careful word. And to stand with these tattered refugees, to pretend to be one them in front of the Cecil, mocks all that I am, had been actually. And will never be again. I could not look at the entry to the hotel, not only because I might be recognized but because the flood of memory could bring the wash of tears. There I had gone with Balthazar, my friend who would betray me because blood and history are deeper than friendship. There he had introduced me to her, the exotic fauna in the shoes worn without hose under a skirt and tunic of cotton suited more to a merchant's café on the Cornice than to this carpeted and mirrored lobby with its potted palms and white gloved attendants, deferential, glad to be of use. Though she smelled of patchouli and what a writer friend called 'the ammoniac smell of the great queens,' a writer friend who was more fond of his words than that tear making odor. She was what I needed—or what Balthazar told me I needed. She could assure the Jewish conspirators in Palestine that I was not merely a rich Copt playing at politics. After all, if I were to marry a divorced Jew, risk all, my social life, my family's own safety, might I not risk even more to arm these same Jews in Palestine? They alone, young and vital, stood against the British imperialism of the past and the Moslem dominance of the future. We Copts would gamble all on an alliance with these Jews with their claim to rights as ancient as our own. We might as well have tried to break the bank at Monte Carlo as trust the Zionists to protect this now obscure Christian sect. We had indeed lost our past security and would, without doubt, lose even more. We would not, as I now knew, find a place in a Moslem Egypt nor a Zionist Israel. As they had been victims, so would we be. Compassion seldom accompanies victory, and they would not only take the land of the Palestinians, they their homes as well. Keys to those lost houses would forever figure in the art of the wandering Palestinians.

With the plot revealed, the Jews in possession of the weapons, Memlik Pasha, Secretary of the Interior in this new Moslem government, draining my blood and treasure, and the war upon us, I avoided those in the Cecil, those who had envied me, who would now have relished spurning me. By then, the British had made the Cecil their base in Alexandria, Alex on the wrong side of the Med to those Helinophiles, and that pompous ass Montgomery who had emptied the upstairs bar of alcohol and turned it into his war room. Daily he marched through the lobby in those baggy shorts with the swagger stick under his arm entered the bird cage of the elevator and barked out: 'The war room, if you please.' If you please indeed. Egypt had not done as it pleased since the British High Commissioner began to govern Egypt after the First World War. Probably even earlier, supplanting what should have been Egypt's middle age with colonial subservience. Our history and culture had been subjugated to archaeological curiosities and mementos removed by rape and deposited in the museums of towns in England as well as stacked in the British Museum along with such stolen trophies as the Elgin Marbles. The Brits took what they wanted, women, cultural artifacts, buildings, our self respect, the grandeur of our civilization and left us as no more than plunder for petty and venal political predators, of whom the Memlik Pasha included me among his prey."

The drive from Alexandria to Wadi al Natrun should take less than two hours. In the wounded and worn creature that carried the pilgrims at least twice that. None talked to another. None read a newspaper, magazine, or book. The flotsam and jetsam of the war that washed up in Alexandria had silence and invisibility beaten into them. Peace did not bring a change, only at best the memory of dashed hopes. At least one had fought with the French Resistance on the Communist side and had watched as De Galle rode triumphantly into Paris, obliterating their hopes. Unlike some who stayed, attended youth conferences that promised a new day, he drifted ever south and away from lost hopes and dreams. Not unique by any means, he was one of those who found in Communism a religion that fed his desire. The dream died not only because of Stalin's purges but because France herself tossed away equalité and fraternité. The old families, some well established before the Revolution, said it cut the ties with the past as the blade cut the heads, yet still owned their factories and summer houses. Now, this lost derelict, this refuge from war and Communism, in a suit gathered from a hostel in Athens, while its owner slept off wine, had no reason to contemplate a society in which the hungry would be fed, the talented would be rewarded, the good lovers would be mated, almost a just world. For him, bread itself had been the great equalizer. Though he could not but think: "God made men and bread separated them." The smell of fresh bread from a Parisian bakery stayed in his nostrils calling to mind the distance. Perhaps this old religion of his youth would be the solace of his last years. He could have whatever he could find as his due. I, too, your intrepid narrator, know how smell lingers in the deepest crevices of the self had been fortunate to walk past a bakery in Provence that smelled of baguettes and to walk the streets that wound back from the Vidroule. Roman legionnaires had walked by this river as victors and I walked there, though as a recluse not as one who had seen the enemy and been destroyed by him. War leaves few unmarked.

Few on that bus had even a piece of bread left from the morning breaking of the fast, though their enforced fast was longer than one night. It stretched back into those years of deprivation when torn from their lives they fled before the war. Few got away, none on the bus with its leather seats replaced by wicker, its 6 hp engine oozing oil, its bearings complaining, and certain to join the other dead machines of the war as a testimonial to the desire of our species to build a barrier between us and the certainty of death. Ironically, we do so by killing millions. But when the bus stopped in front of the monastery, these poor emptied out in little knots, holding their maps of the main church. Clucking like chickens released into the barnyard, unaware of the ever present ax.

Their distress had little purchase in Nessim's mind as he reflected: "I could have wished a memory other than of the farmyard to come again, bringing with it Karm Abu Girg. I had stood there in front of that rambling stuccoed house with its well and stables while the chickens gathered in little knots. They sought bits of grain on earth bare as my memory, yet it fed hopes wired into their being by the ages of the dream that they would only be here if their hopes were real. Those hopes fled when Narouz's horse scattered the ever hopeful hens. He alighted and carried the broken body of our father from the gharry into the house. Though alive, he would never walk again and would grow in bitterness. A secular Copt and desert lord, Faltaus would still find belief outside the church as he had before, believing not in any god, believing only in his land, his wife, his sons. For he needed belief, something to hold to as he held onto the memory of the Coptic illustrious past: lords of the kingdom, keepers of the history of Egypt, and descendants of those who cared for the Holy Family. Even these memories of their Egypt trembled into a shadow as the British found nothing to be gained from an obscure Christian sect and left them to whatever life we might have in a Moslem world. We would find little and would become, in time, refugees from yet another pogrom. Falhus would die before he would see this end, the chickens plucked, roasted, and served on a platter. My father betrayed and betrayer."

Nessim would with passion spent recall what that most bank clerkly of Englishmen wrote: "Time present and time past/Are both perhaps present in time future." Removed as he could be and was, Eliot could live so, even after the London Blitz, even after all the deaths, even of that Frenchman who died in the so called Great War. For Nessim, though, in a desert that lacked a

Museum Pub and a comfortable room of his own, he had instead this Coptic holy place struggling against the ocean of sand and the rising force of Islam with its present and future empty hopes. Only the past was real. The brown and white chickens that scattered under the wheels of the enclosed carriage intended to bring back mother and wife to her family, back from her visit with the Harouns, the Jews who lived in that fortress with its terraces, out buildings housing retainers and a family of husband wife, sons. Faltaus and Narouz with Felim, the most faithful retainer, had come to escort Leila back to Abu Greig, her prison without bars. She was the Dark Swallow who had flown into the unknown arts of Europe, who had been the dark star not only of her Egypt but of all the places she rested and hoped to live. But her parents had tightened the nets, pulled her back to a life she loathed. In that closed world of Coptic Egypt, she had been given in marriage to the old man, taken from her life in the capitals of Europe, from a life that could have mattered, had been given in married servitude to live in a crumbling farm with her books in French, in English, her only intelligent companions. She had not even music. But she did have resentment for the son who could escape if only to Alexandria, though not only there. For he would be torn from Egypt by her dreams, the conflicted emotions of desire and hatred, which would spread out from her in a web that would destroy them all.

But now Nessim stood in the courtyard while his father was carried into the house. Nessim had ridden the horse left for him at the ferry. He could not know Felim would soon take the ferry and the waiting car to Alexandria, returning with a doctor who would fail to make Falhus whole or even relieve his pain or his anger. The dogs had started up a desert wolf, and in the heat of the chase, his horse had fallen. The horse rose and walked. Falhus did neither then and would never do so again. And Leila would give him neither salve for his bodily pain nor ease for his broken manhood. Instead she would give him shame and obsession. This memory came at a moment in which hens fluttered, a moment of emotions and memories so different from what should have occurred in this place where Joseph and Mary rested with the infant benison of the world. Could ever again this uprooted man feel the peace that passes understanding, the peace that purpose brings?

"Do you need help, brother? Or are you just lost in thought in this holy place?" Turning to face the calloused hand that held his wrist, Nessim saw a man whose survival had been heavily paid for: emaciated, some teeth gone, and a scar across his face that recalled the whip. And his accented French recalled any of several places in the Balkans. Or so Nessim thought. Actually, he was French but had lived too hard and deep for years where French could bring reprisal or at least suspicion. "A moment's epiphany, my friend, of my own less than holy family," Nessim said without the wry smile of complicity that would have called forth a response. Nessim knew the man later would wonder but soon forget why he did not return on the bus with the rest of them. Any conversation could provide a clue, and he did not know this broken remnant of the war or who broke him and why. Alexandria since the time of the boy king had been a place of intrigue and deception, a way of life he now hoped to flee. He would forget even the child prostitutes who decorated the walls of their room with blue hand prints to protect them from the evil eye and malevolent spirits. They seemed unaware that the evil in the pants of men was what they had to fear, an evil that would cast them away before they grew hair on their bodies. Or grew teeth to replace the early ones that had fallen out or been knocked out. They would not live long enough to know the nature of an evil which Nessim had learned by their age and survived by feeding it. A quick ducking of his head gave Nessim shade to cover the unmasked eye. His questioner had noted the eye already, stored it away for use as he had stored away knowledge of hidden treasures of fellow internees to be traded for a bowl of soup or a day's reprieve from the whip, thinking that all have a breaking point in a time and place with only survivors not heroes. Always he would be a spy.

But now if he would be a spy, he would be one in the house of the Lord. For he and the other pilgrims moved through the open doors of the walls that enclosed the monastery. For the nine, the enclosure was novel as would be the church, though not the sounds of worship if they heard them: the muted sounds of hand held instruments, triangle and such, or the swirling incense, the small loafs of bread with the Coptic cross on feast days. The quiet awe that filled the main church came not only from the sacredness of the place itself but from the body of St. Bishoy undefiled after centuries of rest. They would touch their heads to the glass that held in state the body, touch with their heads the glass front of the shrine itself, touch it where the small slippered feet could be seen, and murmur their prayers. For those who were believers, and not all were, the experience would be transformative, and they would be forever changed, devout but not perhaps more decent or moral. But then does the soul's enlightenment change the flesh and blood it inhabits? Such thoughts of flesh and belief were not of them as they walked in light filtered by dust motes centuries old it would seem.

For all but the man in the bespoke suit, none had been here before. Nor would they ever be here again. Their pilgrimage would end here. His had begun here a year ago. As his earthly treasures declined, his enforced need for them declined as well. Even before puberty, he had been bred to acquire what the world could give of its treasure and the pomp of circumstance that would attend them. Acquire them he did, the elegantly modern town house, the Silver Ghost with the daffodil hubcaps, the obeisance and envy of his fellows, the veiled hatred of his mother. And all would be so bitter to him that he was sure his flesh if dried and eaten as was mummia would be immediately disgorged not swallowed in joy, not tasting at all like Bombay duck as did mummia.

His worldly decline came as he was found to be a conspirator in the Coptic plot to arm the Irgun in Palestine, perchance to find a protected recluse in the world of Islam that would come with the departure of the British. After all, though their claim was ancient, the Jews now in Palestine had the fervor of a people seeing the Promised Land for the first time. Bred to believe, Nessim did not question the reality of his dream, just as the Jews did not question theirs. Memlik Pasha, minister of Interior in the new Egypt, drained away his money, his Silver Ghost, the trappings of his house, and left only the house ringing with echoes to assure that he would have, for the time being, a gradual decline into a rather comfortable penury rather than prison and torture. The Minister even acquired his wife, the least treasured of Nessim's worldly holdings, and would have her until she, too, could disappear, probably into a kibbutz where, if there were a God, she would grow more hag like every day. And Nessim, finally rid of Justine, would try not to recall her in his friend's wife Eve, also Jewish and of Alexandria.

Nessim, neither of Egypt past or present, reflected: "Three years ago, I sat in the Long Bar in Shepherd's just to watch the English soldiers, some in their Desert Rat shorts and shirts, some in regimental dress, some mere governmental staff. All were gathered here where only men drank to deny with alcohol and each other their exile in Egypt and the fear that preceded the advance of Rommel's tank corps now not far from the railroad station of El Alamein. Still with both eyes and dressed to be comfortable in a London club or a British bar, I watched as she liberated the Long Bar. Though she could have gone to the American Bar and been served conventionally, Lee Miller, chose to be the first woman to set foot in this room that smelled of cheap cologne and dried sweat, entered with assurance: 'Alright, which of you chaps is going to buy me a drink.' Stunned, all except one stood carved in stone. The exception was a quite short man, handsome with his haired bleached to 9 karats and his suit a bit in need of attention: 'My dear, if that's all you require, every man in this room will buy you a drink. If your needs are more of the flesh, I recommend myself.' Undeterred by her assurance that she needed only a drink because she was well serviced by her husband, with a smile of dejection but not of despair, Larry called to the barman: 'Joe, a Suffering Buzzard for our new friend.' He then left her to be entertained by a mustached major whose cheap cologne announced he was assuredly not recently on a tank in the desert."

Turning to Nessim with amusement, he surprised him by recalling his name. They had met only once, at a formal dinner given by the new ambassador, Mountolive, at the British Embassy. Nessim the lone Copt in a room with fifty or so Brits and Egyptians was there only because his mother, Leila, had once been the lover of Mountolive when he was a junior in the diplomatic corps. Not enough to get Nessim close to the Ambassador, he found himself at a back table with a few of the slaveys of the Embassy. One of whom was a junior information officer named Lawrence Durrell.

Recalling his previous meeting, this most interior of men again reflected: "We had sat in the room ablaze with light and looked out the open doors to where the soft green lawn sloped down to the Nile. Ambassador David Mountolive had been seen reclining on that lawn late at night wearing his white cotton pajamas and smoking a cigarette. We did not find either room or lawn relaxing and turned away from both to discuss a shared topic, London and its writers. That I had once or twice sat in the office of Eliot and that I was not Arab gave me purchase; for Eliot was Durrell's mentor, and he considered Egyptians 'gorillas in nightgowns.' Later when we met for coffee at Pastroudis, he gave me a copy of his novel, *The Black Book* about London which was a part of the England he disliked and hoisted not on a petard but on a sharp insult. I thought: 'Good Lord, if this is how he treats places he dislikes, I hope he never writes about Alexandria.' I found the portrayal of bohemian life in London only slightly leavened by humor. But we shared a love of books. I because they took me away from life and he because they involved him in life, even life that turned even his indelicate stomach. But now we dabbled through the guinea fowl, the potatoes both roast and steamed, as is the British fashion, the crisp green salad, the pudding, at which Larry turned up his nose. He did enjoy, excessively, the wine and the brandy after, both rare and French. I drank some of all to be polite only. No more than by woman's flesh did I delight in the other feasts of the flesh. Not much has changed, as I bow my head to new purpose and meaning.

"We walked together with Pursewarden, his fellow writer and slavey, after the dinner, I towards my own glittering house, Durrell to the tower he occupied with constantly changing and eddying women who provided what he called Alexandria's provender of flesh. He had but sampled a meager first course when his wife said, 'Enough.' She and their daughter left for Palestine, which would be her salvation and my damnation. Perhaps, life does serve us what we need. What Pursewarden seemed to want from life was easily found in Alexandria. In the small café where we stopped to talk, I had coffee, Larry brandy, and Pursewarden absinthe. Before we left, he and the Green Fairy were fairly wed."

The poetic moment detached from the surly demands of narrative, leads rather than follows, assuming its centrality of what and who we are, not just beings whipped by a linear truth. Leading us to know time and space are but a stream to drift upon. All mystics, surrealists, and artists who dip their toes in eternity know this. I, too, go where the stream carries me, mostly, though at times I can dream a course for myself. And sit on the porch swing with my grandmother watching the clouds build up over the low hills of Appalachia. Other times, I can stand by a pillar in the conference room at the University of Alexandria talking with Edwar al-Kharrat after he has spoken about how little Lawrence Durrell understood Alexandria and its citizens. I tell him I knew Larry and had thought how he might have responded. As I grip Edwar's left arm, Larry speaks in my left ear words that I mouth: "My dear friend, my beloved fellow writer, you are exactly right. I have not written about your Alexandria, but you have not spoken about mine," in his rather posh and plumy voice not my flat American one. Or I could be in the Alexandria of 1943 but not among the Europeans and the wealthy Alexandrians. But with the young Edwar coping with desire and worshipful dumbness.

Nessim, as well, finds his mind drifting upon the stream of eternity, stopping at his own island, as he moves with the others on the eternity of this sacred place: "For now I am in the main church at the Monastery of St. Bishoy. The smell of incense lingers, recalling what had brought me here. Even now in this sanctuary, the aroma of incense lingers and pulls me into the eternity of this place, almost but not quite overcoming the imprint of patchouli and women's musk. Her smell is a tie to the past, to the secular life that was torn and drained from me from the early rape by Tinki, to the draining of my treasure as a sop to a safety I fear and do not expect. What did the poet say: 'A man who is with wife and child has given hostage to fortune?' Perhaps when young I should have thrown my seeds into the belly of whores rather than my mind into books and causes doomed and imaginary.

"I can hope, though in vain I am sure, that who I was will be of a forgotten past as much as the old bespoke clothes I exchange for those of a Coptic monk. Clothes that cost me more than ever I gave to a Savile Row tailor, the robe and hood, braided belt that I would shed and become once again a secular being with even less interest in God than I had in the desert with its infamies and degradations and defeats. They will burn quietly, though not with a gem-like flame, even in the depthless night. And I will guard them carefully imprisoned in memory lest they reveal selves best dead. Would that I could say of them as I do of that ineradicable memory of her whose teeth are forever gnawing at my *amour proper:* 'But that was in another land and besides the wench is dead,' as Christopher Marlowe once immortalized for all men who find themselves alone and like it so."

CHAPTER TWO

All our paths led from and to the same place. Yet our paths were found not by choice but by what we need and want or what we can no longer live with. For the three of us, Alexandria was not a place but a time schemata, each of us overlapping the other but each of us caught in what marked us. And marked the place, of course, if a difference exists.

Though the wind had blown away the hoof prints and no sign of the boy or the horse could be seen, Felim knew where the horse had carried Nessim. The boy was simply fleeing the compound with no thought of quiet confessions or where he wished to go since he only wanted to be away from the screams of his mother in labor. And being neither a natural horseman nor one on whom training made him a skilled one, he would go where the horse wished to go. And the horse Felim had saddled for himself shortly after dawn would go to water, as would any desert bred being. The boy was desert born but not desert bred. Like his mother, he was of the town and belonged to books, cafes, clothes that smelled of cologne. What little he understood of the desert would never make him at ease with the smell of horse and rider, the illiterate musings of those who lived in the desert, who ate meat cooked over an open fire and drank tepid and often murky water. He would be of the paneled board room not the tent, the motor car not the horse, the song of a chanteuse in a quiet club not the scream of a woman giving birth after two days in labor while the midwife whimpered in the dark corner of the room and the bemused doctor watched the woman's agony.

Nessim, then as he spoke with Durrell, was drawn back into those dark memories: "This was the most my father had spoken to me in a very long time, though once he had said more to his slender and finely featured son. That was when he still thought I might be desert bred, would learn to love life with a horse and gun, would squat beside the men who worked for us and talk of land and horses smoking a cigarette and perhaps accepting a drink of arak from a pocketed flask. Soon Falhus understood he had only supplied the sperm for his wife's child. Leila would send me to the French boarding school in Alexandria, not to some Coptic school where priests would imbue me with the ethics and beliefs of their arcane religion which she regarded as little more than an obscure cult. In L' Ecole Française, I would at least learn to read the books she loved, though the French priests and tutors would ignore Proust, willing only to be as current as Hugo. She would meet me there, and we would have meals and tea at the Cecil, the only hotel she would inhabit when visiting Alexandria. Its 'international' clientele, which meant European, allowed her imagination to recreate her own youth, though the Cecil provided but a tawdry imitation. Yet still it recalled the terraces of Le Dōme, La Coupole, the music of Le Bal Negre; for Paris was always her reality. She had lived for some time in rooms overlooking Les Gardens de Luxembourg on the Left Bank and walked daily along the shaded paths, past the small lake where children sailed their boats, sat on the iron benches and watched women sweep by in dresses short enough to bring a blush to her. She was still the young woman of Coptic modesty and ignorance, though she did wear a dress, from time to time, that almost rose to her knees. That dress led to her being recalled to Egypt. But that is a story too ridiculous to tell." Nessim, paused. As he sank into these thoughts, his eyes half shut, he was somewhere in that desert not with me in a Cairo bar.

As he would say to me a bit later, shaking his head, "Durrell, you have seen how she is with the Europeans, especially the British. She shares my father's view of all of you, that you have sacrificed the Copts to the Moslems to create dissent, to weaken Egypt, make it easier to control. Though she appealed to the adventurers who drifted through here in search of wealth or escaping confinement, she was neither of them nor interested in them. Yet she did not reject their advances, but stored away their names and weaknesses for further use. Her smile with them, some would call Sphinx like, suggested an understanding that granted her authority. I was long in learning why." I then understood why I found this attractive woman repellent. I was but a cipher to be totted up on her abacus.

Though a lowly secretary of the British government, I might rise enough to be of use. But of what use then I could not imagine. I would find out and watch her sons decline into one who was clearly mad and one who was lost in her dreams of exceptional life. But these thoughts were interrupted by Nessim's voice: "Still young enough to have a hairless body, I came to Abu Greig for the Easter holiday, away from French texts and the sight of women seen only in the rectangles in the black cloth that showed them to be little more than corpses, eyes lined with kohl, eyes that lighted briefly on my not quite Western and not quite Egyptian face, on my short blue jacket and grey trousers mandated by my school. The sprawling souk drew me but did not accept me. No water carrier offered me water and no seller offered me the sticky sweet or the round cylinder of cane others bought. There I found life that, though I did not understand, smelled of humanity not of books and chalk and old French priests in musty black who though they did not render unto Caesar they did tithe to Caligula.

"At the river crossing I left the car in which I had ridden for the horse Felim had brought with him. And within two hours I stood in the courtyard watching my father lay his whip across the back of a servant who had stolen bread. Neither my father nor the servant made a sound, my father because the whip spoke for him, the servant because his mouth was tied shut on a piece of wood as the tears ran down his cheeks as the blood ran down his back. My mother was in her rooms that for others would be a harem but for her was a bedroom, lounge, and study. There she had tea sent to her from Paris to drink with newspapers from London, Paris,

Madrid, occasionally Berlin. And there when I entered a few days before Easter and a few days before my seventh birthday, I met her only friend Elizabete Rubin Haroun. She like my mother was in exile from all they considered civilized. At her side was her twelve-year-old-daughter Tinki, a child only in years, feral except for her appearance and her frail attempts to sip tea like a lady to be. Her eyes and her teeth that bared when she smiled told of the carnivore even more than did her eyes that regarded me with scorn. To escape the cultural vacancy of Abu Greig, I was to spend my holiday with these Jewish friends of my mother.

"Leila, putting down her cup of tea, told me of her plans: 'There you will see what life should be, fine china, maids to serve meals other than vast joints, You will see what a European school can mean, can do to make one civil, conversant, as is Tinki. Perhaps you too will go to a school in England, a public school with the sons of nobles and learn to be other than an imitation of life itself. You need not unpack. You go with Tinki and her mother and then back to the French priests. Perhaps, the Haroun boys will spend time with you, though they are older than you and also attending school in England. We will talk later when I come to Alexandria.' I did not know then that she was pimping me out to that little bitch Tinki and her family.

"When Tinki first came into my room, I thought she had come by error but soon though bewildered knew she had come to teach me what my mind still considers forbidden, that my body can betray me or be wronged. Between her attacks, through tears, in what she called pillow talk, she told me how she at ten years of age had her childhood stolen. She had been taught well from a family friend, who often came to dinner and stayed for days. The first time he came into her room after the house was asleep, she thought he had confused her room with his own. Then when he turned back her bedding and lifted her little girl's pink night gown, she again thought he had mistaken her room—but for whose? When he entered her she would have cried out in pain if he had not held her mouth shut with his hand. The next time he came into her room, he did not keep her mouth closed. In time this friend of her parents taught her at ten what he had learned in his forty years. Her mother and father, even her brothers, only saw the well-dressed, affluent friend, not the man who preyed on the very young. But Leila was under no such delusion. What she saw in the man's eyes and manner told her she could trust Tinki to warp her own Nessim, turn him into a dissolute whom she could command before he left for the world from which she had been exiled; for surely this delicate, intelligent child needed what the desert knew not of, the life of cafes, books and music, the smell of good shops, the odor of pâté and the taste of grand crus wines. All this she could give or hold back. She did not envision me becoming a secular monk. Nor did she envision that I would find a use for her own repressed life.

"I came to the breakfast room in the morning wary of Tinki and avoiding the eyes of her parents and brothers: 'This young Copt has yet to know the ways of those who know how life is lived on the right side of the Med. Let us hope he will enjoy, or at least not decline, the Seder.' Only then did I understand that I had been sent to this home because the family was Jewish as well as European, because my mother wanted me to know their ways. And those ways of Passover would forever color my own Easter.

'Seder, Passover? Are those part of your Easter celebration? At home, we always have roast lamb, lentils cooked with onions, and fruit from the orchard. Do you do the same?'

'Oh, no, my little Copt,' said Tinki. 'We are Jewish and do not believe in the birth, death, and resurrection of your Savior; for ours is yet to come. What we celebrate at this time of year is the Exodus of our people's time of slavery in Egypt. We celebrate our freedom and our hopes for the land to be once again called Israel.'

'But you are still in Egypt and clearly not in slavery. Look at this house, your clothes, the way you live. Like the rich I see in Alexandria when I go with my mother to the Cecil for tea. You have not left Egypt.'

"I never forgot their laughter as they considered who should explain briefly and clearly the Jews time in Egypt, their slavery by the pharaohs, God's deliverance of them, and their Exodus. He sat wide-eyed as they told him about Moses, of finding and losing their home, of the scattering of the Jews around the world, which they called the Diasporas. And of their struggle to reclaim the land granted them by God, Israel, which would be reclaimed, violently if need be, from the English, from the Moslems, from any and all who held as their own what belonged only to the Jews.

"I sat there among these Europeans, as I thought of them, blank faced and wide of eye, unblinking and probably open-mouthed. Nothing had prepared me for this breakfast of fruit and yogurt, dark rich coffee with cream, and long slender loafs of bread called baguettes, all served by an older Arabic woman, but of the town. She wore a dress of linen with a neck line that showed the tops of her breasts, Western clothes, and her hair was styled in what Mrs. Haroun called a French twist.

"The Master, the husband, spoke at breakfast: 'This evening is the first night of Passover, and we have the Seder, the dinner commemorating the Exodus. We will have songs and prayers and will explain to you why we eat what we will. Though a Gentile, you will be welcome to share this most Jewish of meals, though you will be even more welcome if you are circumcised. But that we will not ask.' Though Tinki kept her head bowed over her breakfast, her curled lips said much to me. I spent much of the day with Ben and Saul, the sons home from England for Passover. They were decent chaps, to use their vernacular, who taught me a bit about cricket, though not about the purpose of the game or the meaning of a sticky wicket or a googly. They did not tell me much that I would learn on my own later: where to buy good clothes in London, how to behave in a London club. I would find acceptance in good clubs easier than they did. For the Brits even a Copt was more acceptable than a Jew. When I told them I doubted that I would ever walk English streets, that my mother would keep me tied to Abu Greig, they smiled and said: 'She has already chosen your public school, a place called Chapterhouse. Be careful there for romance among boys at such schools is commonplace. And you had best avoid those for whom buggery guides them, not the Lord God Almighty.' They laughed when I asked what they meant by buggery. The time I spent there passed in much the same way though Tinki continued her attacks. Durrell, my friend, I hope my halting tale of childhood has not kept you while we watch the sun settle below the horizon and…"

"I know, the 'Evening is laid out against the sky like a patient etherized upon a table,' as my mentor and occasional editor wrote."

"Eliot, ah yes. I spent an afternoon once in a quiet little Bloomsbury flat while that most bank clerkly of Englishmen and his friend Ezra drifted through literature with one reading a translation from the Chinese and the other a draft of *Prufrock*. I never met either again, though I did once see Eliot leaving a café with his wife. He was a bit disheveled. She was quite a bit more disheveled, weeping and clinging to his arm. That he was married took me by surprise, so quiet and distant a man. I never saw him or his wife again. And you, how did you find him?"

"We corresponded mostly, though we often discussed my writings in his office when I could not avoid London. He said to me: "Durrell, be a writer of poetry or fiction. Do not to try both for then two things are done badly," belying his own view. He has continued to publish my poetry and would have published *The Black Book* if it had been publishable in England. I could not neuter it or even tame it enough to make publication possible. He did what could be done and wrote well of me and Miller, earning for himself the appellation on one who 'does dirt' on literature. Pudding Island will not change unless the French take it by scruff and scrotum and give it a good shake, risking even the decorously raised luke warm eye brow. I can't imagine the French would ever trouble themselves. So Miller, Lawrence, and I will continue to be banned and sold only in bookshops catering to readers of the obscene or published only by the French. We'll be in the best of company though. Joyce, course.'

"I remember scenes and phrases from *The Black Book* that caused even me to blanch a bit, and think no wonder the laws of England prevented its being published such insults and mockery on their isle of kings. No wonder the English blanched at the novel. But why would Eliot, who presumed, ineffectually, to be the diffident and proper English gentleman desire to publish *The Black Book*?"

"He saw it for what it is, the story of a religious nervous breakdown. There I finally struggled out of the carapace of all that I was to have been yet had no power to be anything else. I could only rage and hope someday to fly past the nets set to hold me in place."

"I do hope your poetry, not your novel, will be the source of anything you ever write about us, though I cannot imagine we could ever be matter enough for you so we are probably safe."

"Don't be too sure. Well, I must go to Alex and my job in the bowels of the Mission. Thankfully, a dedicated civil servant, more servile than civil, is there to clean my press releases and communiqués or I would soon be teaching those gorillas in nightshirts the basics of English. No, no. Good Herbert will save me from that so that I can translate *The Book of The Dead* into modern Egypt. You may well yourself be fit to start a scene or two. Don't worry, though, I won't strap a codpiece or a set of antlers on you and set you off down the Cornice in that lovely Rolls with its daffodil hubcaps. I'll leave you in that paneled office with the faithful Affad hovering over you and protecting your privacy and reputation.

What would the Ambassador say if he knew you put a spot of rum in your afternoon tea? You could, of course, excuse the excess by borrowing a phrase from my own doctor, the eminent Michel Andorra: 'Sometimes one must find a way to struggle against 'The recurrent anxiety of temporal alignment.'"

The scent of sandal wood, backed by patchouli, struck us so forcibly that while still half risen from his chair he followed the scent to its source—an English correspondent named Keats. And Durrell *soto voce* to me: "What in God's name had brought him to Cairo? Alex is just as corrupt, just as full of lies and whores, though he seems interested only in their clients not their wares. News is where one finds it. Without doubt he will mention my typing failure, leaving out the letter l when released a note, about the French diplomat Pombal who was fined for kissing a woman in public. What I intended as a mild jest became a bit more. Pombal may soon forgive me. But Keats in Cairo, the inescapable and ineffable in a suit better suited for a tout. And with him another civilian, though one of a different cut."

And so seeing us, Keats approached: "Durrell. You in Cairo of all places. With the ambassador due in a week, I expected your time to be spent over a press release not a g and t. That is it, isn't it. I'm just in from Palestine with my friend who is stationed there. Larry, this is Mike Silver. Mike this is Larry Durrell, soon to be but not yet a famous writer. And this is our friend from Alex, Nessim Hosnani. May we join you, or are you about to leave? In which case, may we have your table? Jeeps full of Montgomery's lads will fill this room that is not home but not the desert either."

"We're soon to leave, but do sit. The Mission is abuzz with rumors about Jewish guerrilla bands in Palestine. In your usual snooping under bed clothes, have you anything I can carry back to Alex?"

"Mike is the man to ask, being both Jewish and one of Montgomery's own. I found nothing but sand and gin when I was there, though I did see Nancy briefly." Mentioning Larry's recently departed wife brought a strained silence to the table, not the quotable wry remark or restrained snarl Keats lived to collect in hopes it might prove news worthy. But it did elicit a cough behind his hand from Mike.

"Oh and how is my wife doing? I seldom hear from her." Mike Silver was absorbed in stirring his drink, leaving the conversation to Keats, who replied to Durrell: "Doing well. Working for the Brits, as you know. As in a way, I guess we all are. But getting back to the Jews. It's not just the Irgun, you know, though they seem to have ties with all the groups. Dangerous lot, I think. But again, Mike is the man to ask. What's the gen, old man."

Returning to the conversation Mike said: "I know little about what they do or are, just that they dislike the Palestinians and the Brits. And don't like anyone with ties of any kind to either. Nothing ended a conversation at a café in the Jewish quarter of Jerusalem like mentioning the possibility of an uprising. Being a Jew gave me no bona fides. Only those who have dipped their hands in the blood of the lamb have any purchase, even if they might be useful to the cause of bringing Israel into being. Anyone else, even if useful, might as well be dead. And will be if they are even nuisances. But in the shifting of power in the Levant, they are a constant and here to stay. Make no mistake about that."

"An old India Army general named Masklyne says much the same. We inherited 'the Brig,' as his factotum calls him but not to his face, from the High Commission. He's compiled dossiers on half of Alex and distrusts the other half, upsetting to our presence in the new order. Most see him as quite out of touch with the present, lost in a turbulent past and an uncertain future. I've been compiling my own dossier on the fellow. Nasty bit of work, and he doesn't like me at all. I'm not quite right you know, too friendly with the locals. Like our friend Nessim here. Have you ever chanced to find him hiding in your W.C., Nessim? We will leave to you the table and the lads in short pants. And we'll stretch our legs before returning to Alex after the sun has dropped. Be careful about who you talk with Keats. Unsubstantiated rumors abound. Enjoy your time out of Palestine, Mike, that is if you are here to enjoy yourself."

Our walk from Shepherd's had only the aim of getting away from the tide of khaki moving away from us. So we found ourselves seated on the terrace of a small undistinguished café drinking Turkish coffee with some of those crispy pasties flavored with cinnamon and sugar. We talked about nothing really, just the few spots in London I remembered without distaste and the ones whose names Nessim bore on the inside pocket of his jacket. I interrupted this drowsy distraction with a startled whisper: "Don't look. Just take my word for it. There's a pair of American shoes two tables behind you. What the hell is an American doing here, especially one who is too badly dressed to be rich and too intelligent, I think, to be a diplomat. He's utterly lost in whatever he's writing. I'm sure he'll respond to my most British and plumy voice: 'I say there, young American. Would you care to join us for a coffee?'"

The young man who came to our table was thin, in need of all care, and wearing the distracted air of someone who really didn't give a damn. But he came, sat down, accepted the coffee, turned down the offer of a pastis and introduced himself: "I'm Charles Robertson. And you're right. I am American, and as you obviously think I am deservedly down on my luck. I hope the cut of your clothes indicates that you are deservedly fortunate, if such is possible." Durrell with a smile laced with irony replied: "I am an unworthy member of the British government, but my friend here is an Egyptian on whom God has bestowed wealth." Though he had been in Egypt long enough to know something, the young American could make no fine distinctions and failed to here: "You mean Allah, don't you?" Correcting him, Durrell also introduced himself: "Oh no. My friend is a Copt, Nessim Hosnani. I am Lawrence Durrell." With a bit of life to him, Robertson found entry into the conversation that would cast his lot forever: "I know of you from my friend Miller and the beauteous Anais. I was in Paris as a copy editor for an American news service. I stayed after the Villa Serat gang moved south to Greece or west to America, too long actually to get back to the States. Someday I'll write about the way out, which had much in common with the way in, by chance, and by hook and by crook. As my grandmother would say before saying she hoped I would avoid being hanged."

Of course unaware of what he would set in motion, Durrell replied: "So you are a writer, a member of the most impoverished aristocracy that ever lived. Lost in this desolate world of gorillas in night shirts and soldiers in battle gear in this empire of sand with only memories of its past, no middle life and no present. Nothing to accept much less sustain a life other than one of greed, avarice, and, fortunately, a sexuality of astonishing variety." He apologized to Nessim who had by now withdrawn into his own thoughts: "Sorry, Nessim." And turned to hear what Robertson had to say: "A writer? Not yet, but I write. Just now, I'm trying to understand a scene from my childhood. I was young, a child of the American mountain range called Appalachia. A place of violence, clannish and inbred with men and women lost in loyalties so visceral, so at odds with the very human desire to live that a violent rejection of loves or of another is impossible. But I drift. Walking in the hills I came upon the dead body of a raccoon, so long dead that maggots crawled in it. Curled up against it was a young raccoon, called a kit. You've probably never seen one, an attractive member of the rodent family. This one has thumbs. The kit, like its mother was covered with maggots and unable to move. I stained a stick in animal pail shocked to realize I knew no one for whom such natural bonds exist. Even though the kit was destroyed, its only hope was the family. A simple way our species either never had or cannot achieve again. I fail to write more about this mountain moment. Perhaps I can if I get close enough to life itself to understand why a world that exists to sustain life should give life to a species that seems to exist to destroy itself if necessary by destroying all that sustains it. I have written an inkling of a simple life, a simple path perhaps, though one that is fragile, tenuous—to much so to continue." Recognizing a man sharing his own discomfort with life itself. Durrell said: "You own thoughts too deep for comfort, young friend. Let's hear what you have." In quiet voice that still carried the nasal twang of Appalachia, he spoke:

'Not even the three day closing of the mines
cleared the creek which would run black from the collieries' spillage
for a week after a strike began d certainly couldn't be cleared by Easter
and not even my grandmother's good blue dress
changed her farm woman's body bent and off center
and her gnarled hands shaped her white gloves
touched the road we walked for 2 miles up and across the hill
past the cemetery, the movie house, The Methodist church
to the red brick and white pillars of her church
and not even my new suit and shoes
touched the soul of me that wanted
the hills with their spring blooming of dogwood and violet
that wanted to stay as straight as my trouser's crease
as white as my shirt, as spotless as my shoes
not even the organ and the choir leading us to sing
'up from the grave he arose
With a mighty triumph o'er his foes'
brought me to dedicate my life to the pale Jew

the avatar whose domain was falling
to roads and politicians and snot nosed kids
who knew too much.'

"If you have no reason to stay here, let's pick up your kit and go to Alex. I can use someone who can think and write at the Mission. Oh, and can you type?"

CHAPTER

THREE

Nessim stayed on in the café after his companions left for Alexandria. Though a whore to those who had bought her and destroyed her, to Nessim she was the city founded by the boy king, the jewel of the lost empire, not the international market for cotton and whatever else the Europeans would pay for, reducing the cotton brokers of his city to well paid servants. Servants who would sit by the door of their masters in hopes of a bone or a piece of bread in the form of British pounds or French francs. She was not even a memory of the Egypt in which the Copts were valued as advisors to pharaohs. If they could not again see that Egypt, with the help of the Jews, they would at least find a place at the table above the salt, so to speak. And so he sat lost in the dream of a dead past and in what he would soon know was an equally vain expectation of the future. He sat waiting for his unnamed Jewish contact who was then cleaning guns just received from Krupp.

Having heard from informants in British intelligence that the trap was closing on the Copts, the Irgun would take what they had and disappear into the desert. Knowing none of this, yet Nessim understood that the Copts had lost. And that he should return to Alexandria to save what he could.

The great desert was lighted only by the headlights of the Rolls and perhaps a bit by the Hair of Berenices stuck in the darkness above. No light at all salved his dread of loss as he thought back to beginning of the "great" plot. Leila, embittered by a Europe as lost to her as was the greatness of the Coptic past, devoted her cunning and shrewd mind to what might be saved: the Copts who would surely be lost in the tide that was then emerging, a Moslem Egypt. Here, at least, was a subject that took her beyond the crumbling walls of her prison, beyond the company of her fellow prisoners, the old cobra that drank milk from a saucer and her husband wrapped in robes in his wheel chair. A visit with Sara Haroun led to Leila's meeting a stocky man in his fifties with grizzled hair and a willingness to meet with her alone. In exchange for guns, he offered safety for the Copts in the new Levant, especially Egypt. She believed, both needed and desired to believe, that these intense and driven Jews who defied the British restriction on immigration would be the light and the power when their state came into being, probably at the expense of the Moslems. Her son, Nessim, would be her banker and her voice. He could be where she could not. She would toil in her bed with the young British diplomat Nessim brought to visit them a few weeks ago, David Mountolive. In time, he might be useful, and she would keep him inside her robe with all her wit and wiles. Such thoughts came to Nessim as he felt the plot lose identity and cause him to wonder if Leila could salvage anything when she met again with that British Diplomat, Sir David Mountolive the newly appointed ambassador to Egypt. Having once been cast in the role of pimp for his mother, he believed she should continue to be of what use she could. Granted, she would not again be in Mountolive's bed, not this old remnant of the desert, this pocked marked survivor of disease, this shrill old woman smelling of patchouli and stale flesh. What had Larry called him, that young diplomat, her Oedipal surrogate? Yes, that was it. And this is now and yet it is of the past, the past that Balthazar also made use of as the scribe and messenger of the plot.

Balthazar both knew all and knew everyone in Egypt, all who and what mattered that is. He was a master of the Cabal, that arcane study of earth and heaven. Devotees met infrequently and for many reasons, some to be seen in the company of the elite, some to turn a profit, some out of devotion. And within that diverse group existed a Coptic few whose plot to rise in the new Egypt or at least to be safe in it needed only the freedom to act. That came to them with the death of Falhus, the old patriarch who lived only in the past, protected by his desert domain from all but his bitterness. That was told to them by Balthazar who knew all and could use all as he needed to further the Jewish state.

That, too, came, quietly at night as Falhus's sleeping draught drained away his life. Narouz found him dead, and the tray with coffee and flat bread fell from his hands shattering with a sound overwhelmed by the cry of this son of Falhus, a cry the mourners would echo later in the day, for by Coptic tradition the memorial service must be quick upon the shadow of the death. Narous, the faithful gun dog, would let no one else in with the dead. Not his mother. Not his brother. Not any of those who had served Falhus all their lives. Only he undressed and washed his father's body and then anointed it with a balm made of frankincense, myrrh, and something else old Anna would never reveal. Narouz then dressed his father in the clothes he had worn long ago when he married Leila. Though the Turkish trousers and the tunic were now too large for the body of his father, Narouz had chosen them not only for the fineness of the material and the care with which they were made but also because they commemorated that earlier ceremony, his father's marriage to his mother.

The body prepared, Narous let in the family, the retainers and the six old women dressed in black, the formal mourners, the ones who would carry to the desert community news of the death. The priest who would officiate at the ceremony was there of course and would lead the small procession to the grave already prepared for Falhus. Those who had come and those who were always there met briefly in the house. Then all was as it had been for so long, silent and even more empty of life. As Narouz watched Nessim and Leila go to the ante room of her harem with a man he had never seen before, a stocky man with grizzled hair and Arabic features, he realized the life he knew was buried with his father. He would continue the struggle against the sand and the salt touched water, striving to turn them into arable land. And he would continue to be a desert wise ruler of his father's kingdom, but he would never be the patriarch or even the dominant figure in their enterprises his father had been. Now his mother and his brother would have that power if not the respect of the life of the desert, a life that had neither interest nor value to them.

Narouz was no longer his father's eyes and ears, the hands and feet that took the old man not only to his property but into the quiet confidences of his wife and his elder son. For though they were careful, they did not know the house itself as did Narouz who had become stealth itself. Little of business and people they conspired with did he understand though he repeated what he heard without comment. The life of their desert holding, of the people whose families had worked there for generations, the horse he had from Assam, these he spoke of with love and passion, giving to his father the smell of the horse's sweat, the pungent odor of the wetlands, the laughter of Assam when the horse fought him. They were real to him and of a different order from the places and people his mother and brother spoke of: a farm in Kenya, investments in Palestine, business dealing in Germany, and banking in Europe as well as the Levant. All this belonged to the office Nessim had not far from the Bourse in Alexandria; which Narouz visited only when Nessim insisted that he sign a document or attend a gathering to feel at one with his younger brother. Of such gatherings, he preferred Carnival when he could hide in a domino, not shrink into shadows as he did in the cafes where Nessim shared with him a life he cared little for. Men with soft hands and brittle laughter, women who smelled of perfume not sweat, few whose manner spoke of the earth and the clannish people whose life dismissed all who were not bred as they were. Except for that odd American, Charles Robertson, and the woman who was with him, known only as Vega, now a nurse at the British Military Hospital. Though he spoke of books and foreign life, his hands still held the mark of labor, a labor different from what Durrell had found for him in the bowels of the Embassy where secrets were hidden and forgotten, where lives were totted up like so many bales of cotton at the market. He, Narous, understood when their hands met, but not when they spoke, for Charles was of places and work that was not of the desert with its oases and thirst.

Yet what separated Charles from Narous, and if truth be told from every living person in Alexandria, did not make him an exile. Far from it. At first, Charles was interesting because of his difference, even a bit exotic. But as he became part of the local fauna, he found a place as the darling of the salon of women who aspired to a culture as different from that of Egypt as the clothes sent to them from Paris. Accustomed to being politely bored by men, and some women, who spoke of life and art they themselves know only from books, Charles brought with him an experience they understood. He told stories he had heard over the fires in work camps, played music on his guitar he had heard in Storyville, stories and songs that said they were not empty and devoid of real life. Though the rich women could not share in such hard scrabble life, they shared its void and loved the man who understood them. At the suggestion of Nessim, Justine went one evening when Charles Robertson was speaking of the migrant worker trail that went from the southern to the northern borders of American, singing the songs of the compasenios who traveled it doing stoop labor during the day and recalling in corredas at night a home far away. That Balthazar had already named Charles as useful prey to Justine who was to find a replacement in the Embassy for Durrell, who seemed too cynically aware to be lured into pillow talk with Justine. Then, too, Durrell's frequent mercurial moods troubled those who plotted, who could not risk another unknown. Charles, with his singular devotion to Vega might well be channeled into use. So cynical were the conspirators of both schemes and love. If all was to be lost, they must at least survive.

Vega, as well, found her place, after the obligatory sniffing by the women to see if she posed a threat and by the men to see if she offered a distraction. Slight of build and quiet of demeanor, she offered neither threat nor diversion. Instead, her quietness was a balm as was her light touch on a troubled mind. Only Justine, whose eyes told of strange sins, remained diffident, perhaps threatened. Though she did not love Nessim, she needed him close and focused on her. For she was not only the Jewish bona fides Nessim needed, she was Balthazar's spy. She would know if and when the plot had lost its last veil. Larry, as Justine and Balthazar knew, had sensed that Nessim's monkish life while married to a woman known both for her profligacy and her soul wrenching sexuality shielded an uneasy conundrum, one the writer in him could sense but not yet name. These inroads into the community of the Brits, Nessim and Justine talked of in the secrecy of the bed. Lying like soldiers sleeping in the field, neither looking at one another nor touching as they talked. Nessim sure of the confidence spoke of his dealings with Krupp, his far founded assets, financial and human, the role of Leila. All this Justine retained as she had earlier retained the desires and interests of men.

What they could not understand was that neither Charles Robertson nor Vega were innocents, almost ciphers. Life had marked them and moved on. He with a now instinctive awareness of lies, tricks, and subterfuge. She as an exemplar of that old maxim that purity of the soul can come either from denial of the flesh or exhaustion of the flesh. On the streets since she was a child, denial was never possible for her. Though her love came from an old soul, her body still retained memories of its use as metal bent will return to an earlier form when beaten.

"We should make them comfortable, at ease. This house is too formal, the Cecil too grand. Ah, I know," Justine said. "Pastroudi's for light refreshment, perhaps elevenses. There we can chat without the dilution of alcohol or the distraction of that which is foreign to them. Yet fitting for anyone who wishes to be seen in the European community. Respect writ small will do."

So Nessim and Justine, Charles and Vega met one weekday morning after Justine had bathed and Nessim had been shaved to talk with and if possible seduce into conspiracy the two bits of flotsam from the war. The dark Turkish coffee was served with bread flavored with cardamom and dusted with sugar and, of course, the small bowl of olives. "You have travelled far, have you then," said Justine as her toe touched the unfashionable toe of Charles' shoe and her dark eyes looked for any sign that he knew she was not bound by any law or custom. He smelt in her the same mock desire of women from the fields or the camps. But they would barter feigned lust for a day away from work. But this rich society bitch: "What could she want of a mere scribe?" Aware, as well, that Nessim's eyes moved easily from him to Vega, he thought as well that these two rich were not merely slumming but needed something that he could not then find. Turning slightly to face Justine, Vega said: "Yes, we have travelled far, from Poland when the tanks moved in to the Balkans then to Avignon where the Milice rounded up the Jews and shipped them like so much fodder to work camps and worse. They would not survive and neither would we if we could not be identified as either complicit or stupidly harmless. Neither was possible. So we found our way to Greece." To Tinos, actually," said Charles, "late in the year of 1940 while the sinking of the Greek destroyer *Elli* by an Italian submarine was like a wound to the people." War had not been declared at the time of the attack, and when they arrived the Greeks were incensed by what they rightly called a cowardly act and swore revenge. They had no way of knowing the devastation of conquest they would face—not without resistance. Vega and Charles found the door to a simple path in this ancient site of healing, despite the war. For they wandered into the memory of an ancient sanctuary. Dedicated to Poseidon and Amphitrite its fame for healing continued into Christian times. Pilgrims came to the Orthodox Church on Tinos to be healed. But for them, the ancient site healed the wounds of being violently wrenched and kicked always south away from the war. But that is too a soul deep for words.

Being actually interested in Vega and Charles, Nessim said, "Then you stayed on Tinos until you came here?" Shaken from her quietness, Vega spoke of their wanderings, to Athens, briefly, and then to Crete where they found safety from the war with a group of resistance fighters led by two Englishmen, one named Paddy and the other Ian. They were travelling there with a captured German officer: "They took us with them assuming, correctly, that we would not survive the conflict between the Germans and the resistance of bands of brigands for the nonce more angered by the Germans than with feuds with each other over slights whose origins were lost." Oddly, the soul deep quiet survived, for them, the conflicts foreign and internecine.

Unleashed by Nessim, Justine moved, more discretely than was her fashion and asked Charles if he would speak with a small group of her friends, perhaps read some of his own writing. Unable to decline, he accepted. Back at the Mission, he sought out Durrell and told him of the contrived hour spent with Nessim and Justine, listening for confirmation of what even he could sense. Durrell eased himself in his chair to look closely at Charles: "If you survive your tryst with the Whore of Babylon, you will surpass the fate of your predecessor, Ludwig Pursewarden. His brief misalliance with her could have cost him his job rather than a transfer to another office. His sister has legs, actual and metaphorical. You may very well meet her since she is now married to our lord and master, Ambassador David Mountolive. It was Pursewarden who said of Justine: 'She is a time worn turnstile through which we are all expected to pass to be part of whatever this is.' He was right, of course. And what this, as he knew, is a place in which sex is devoid of meaning, of feeling of any sort. I chose not to make the passage.

He did. I am here, and he is not. I am inured to such reality, of which as Eliot wrote: 'Humankind cannot bear very much reality.' I advise you travel with care, for you have much to lose." Charles laughed and said: "Much to lose? Have you seen my shoes?" Larry smiled with the sadness of his own life and said: "You have with you Vega, whom Justine will despise, as she does all and everything that reminds her of her own amoral vacuity, any trace of that willingly sold, traces of which ride her like a djinn, forcing her to do ever greater harm." Puzzled, Charles mused and said: "Vega? She is my separate soul. My nurse, my augur. Nothing can touch us."

Just then, Herbert passed by on his way back from lunch holding and embossed envelope which he passed under his nose before dropping it on Charles' desk with the comment: "Such expensive perfume so indulgently presented either hides a secret or is the signature of someone with more money than taste. God save me from either." He sauntered on to his paper littered desk to sort through the morning post as Durrell muttered mostly to himself: "And God save me from such a compulsion to sending," and said aloud: "The sender is most likely both." After slitting open the envelope and scanning the message, Charles looked up and said: "I am invited to give an after dinner talk to a group of women..." and before he could speak further, Durrell said: "At the Cecil. That's her favorite hunting ground. Are you to be paid as well as given dinner?" Charles looked up, stricken but flattered, knowing he was caught and went quietly to his desk where he sat looking at the letter occasionally passing it under his nose. Two days later, he would be shown to a private dining room where only Justine was present. He sat as the waiter opened a bottle of Vieux Clicquot and then left. Much later, he left with another letter in a simple and unscented envelope. This the next day he would pass on to Vega unopened: "The largess of the women who asked me to speak about Eliot's *Four Quartets*. I hope I gave them their money's worth."

That evening, though, he returned to the Embassy where Durrell remained. And looking at Charles without the trace of a smile, Durrell almost whispered: "Whatever you do, change clothes and bathe before you leave. Although there is only a trace of Justine's perfume, there is what the poet called the 'ammoniac smell of the great queens.' You reek of soiled linens." The cluttered office closed in on Charles as he looked at Durrell with neither shame nor surprise but with the relief of one sharing a violation with one who could understand. He was wrong. Though Durrell could write to his friend Henry Miller of "the sexual provender" of Alexandria, the memory of the sun browned wife of Corfu he lost to the war and even earlier to a siren in Paris cloyed the sweetness of his excesses and brought with it a sharp, though sad as well, admonition: "Telling you to consider the cost of Justine's bed will do no good now. Perhaps later."

The door opened suddenly to admit The Brig, as his devoted secretary called him to others, not to his master. Maskylene was Indian Army to the core of his being, strictly a colonial with their devotion to an England that never existed: moral and well meaning, the protector of home and family, the law giver and civilizer of the benighted lands. God help them if they ever saw the real England, tawdry and covetous. Now a remnant of the High Commission, that illegitimate offspring of the old Arab Bureau, he was the military presence at the Mission. Not standing on his usual ceremony, he glared through his monocle at Charles and barked: "Just what the hell are you playing at with that Jewish wife of Hosnani's."

With the bravado of a thief, Charles shouted: "For god's sake, do none of you have nothing to do but sniff my underwear. Isn't there an Empire to protect? Palestine to subvert? Jewish immigration to diminish?"

The Brig with his all knowing smile replied: "Pay your mistress with your puppy like devotion as you massage her toes. Oh yes, that little sign of affection has been noted. Don't pay her with what she and the willing cuckold want and what I cannot tell you and need not. Not until the proverbial fecal matter adds even more stain to your already ignoble self." Trapped, Charles with lips bared, sneered: "What I am 'playing at' as you call it is simply being literary advisor to the Hosnais, who want to build a library. Nothing more." Ball into the court of the Brig: "Surely they could do better than a washed up teacher from America after they did in Pursewarden. Oh, yes, they had a hand in that demotion if that's what it was."

Durrell had listened through his tented finger tips until now. But this vilification of his friend brought about a roar: "Have you no shame at all. As God is my witness, if I can, I will see you shipped out to the darkest hole in the Levant. From there you can spin your lies and theories to anyone there who speaks English." Maskylene turned his monocle towards Durrell, and almost purred: "We will see how long Hosnani's friend, the Ambassador, remains in Egypt when I have the documents I need to tie his friend to the Krupps." Nonchalantly, Durrell ended the exchange: "I would have thought that old nag would have died after you were posted to Jerusalem with a caution."

Adjusting his monocle and brushing away imagined dust from his tunic, the Brig turned on his heel and left, presumably to continue to file his complaints much higher up in the Mission. His chances of actually seeing the Ambassador were slim. Mountolive had known Pursewarden for years and had persuaded him to stay in his position rather than request another assignment, one far away from Maskylene. The two of them had fought often, bitterly, and publicly about Nessim. The glare Maskylene directed at Robertson would have chilled the blood of someone more seasoned than he but did weaken his knees so that he slumped into his chair. And with his head in his hands, he turned to Durrell as the sound of the slammed shut door echoed still and said: "My god, Larry, what have I done."

"You have provided a disturbed mind with raw meat to feed on, a mind tired of mushy peas and roasted potatoes."

"What the hell are you talking about?"

Durrell opened the bottom drawer of his desk, took out a bottle of brandy and two glasses, filled them and gave one to Charles, saying: "This won't help you, but I feel the need. The Brig has compiled a dossier on Nessim seeking to prove that our friend is the central figure in a Coptic plot to arm Jews in Palestine who wish to establish their own homeland there by forcibly deposing the Moslems and ending the British mandate. He is committed to this belief and equally committed to believing that Nessim has infiltrated the British embassy. You have given him what he wanted: a clear connection between Nessim and us. Justine had tried to seduce both Pursewarden and me. We did not actually respond or rather I did not because we thought Maskylene's silly idea has scant merit. We just found her a bit shopworn when Alex has so much fresher women equally attracted to the wee lads who serve the Empire and have access to the Commissary, not that the latter would interest Justine. She simply needs what Nessim does not provide, frequent rogering. Now you, having chosen to dine below the salt, have given him the morsel of proof he wanted. Oh no, no, you won't lose your position here. In fact, he will demand you continue your affair with the dark Justine. You are to be a spy in the house of love." Charles, still holding the untouched glass of brandy, stared at him stupidly, like a deer caught in the poacher's lantern said: "What am I to do?" Idly sniffing his brandy, Durrell said: "You have, already done it. For the love of a woman that can transcend these mortal coils you have accepted in trade a smelly bagatelle." With unaccustomed petulance, Charles almost moaned: "Does everyone, including you, have to make the Taj Mahal out of something as simple as an indiscreet dalliance!!"

Convinced that the Brig was the victim of his own inbred hatred of all who did not revere Blighty, Durrell had decided to accept what amusement he could from the discomfort of all caught in the web. Though here he had from Charles a phrase he would store away like a school boy with a sweet stolen from tea, a sweet that would soon turn acrid.

CHAPTER FOUR

Vega looked with as much skepticism as was possible for someone the Tao had marked and with a muffled sigh moved into the massive building and down the echoing hall to the door with the name Matron. No assistant, secretary, or other being was between her and Miss Miller, Matron. Vega said: "I am Vega. I called about a nursing position."

Miss Miller looked carefully but not without kindness and interest at the slender young blonde woman with the pale violet eyes and the stillness that spoke of an old and wise soul and said: "My dear, are you certain that you want to work here? Or even stay in Alexandria? The German army is almost at the door. We few, we gallant few, are all of the British women left. The WAAFs, the AWRs, the FANYs have been evacuated. Only we are left, members of Queen Alexandra's Nursing Service. And we have been told to keep a suitcase packed in case of immediate evacuation." Looking with equal care at this woman of a tired middle age, Vega said, again with care: "I am here if you need me, and I will stay unless ordered to leave. My training and my first service was at St. Bart's in London and later at the American Hospital of Paris when it once again became a military hospital. Oddly, the insanity of war with its purposeful and meaningless violence has calmed me, led me here, where once more I wish to serve and heal." "Perhaps you will do. If you chose to stay and not pack a suitcase, consider what I have done. Carry a long and strong hat pin and aim for a vital organ as do I," said Matron.

Even in the gloom of that barren, industrial room, Vega paused and passed an almost imperceptible smile and asked: "Do you issue hat pins with our uniforms? I lost my last one when we left Paris in quite a hurry with the German 77s echoing through the streets and shaking the tables at Deux Magots. We left without luggage, a bit damp by the time we got to Gare du Mont Parnasse. And I could see the Germans. They wore gray. I wore blue." Finding common ground, Matron said: "So that is your Paris, the 14th Arrondisment. I remember well staying at the old Select and looking down at the tree Chateaubriand had planted. Are both still there?" Though not really an old Paris hand, Vega could respond: "We stayed a bit on the cheap side at a place without a name on rue Daguerre, close enough to the cemetery to be reminded that the Germans had been there before and that we would do well to leave rather than risk becoming permanent residents."

This exchange of remembrances only began Matron's inquiry: "I have two other concerns: Have you seen so much blood that you will cringe when you are up to your elbows in it and will the other half of your 'we' accept your absence for many hours even many days?" Both questions had the sound of being rehearsed and were. Of the many who came through looking for work or a place to stay, few lasted past the first stream of wounded that at times became a deluge with limbs and organs mere flotsam, testing mind, body, and spirit. "I don't intend to demean or belittle, but you are a bit on the frail side for this kind of work." The mention of frailty brought no smile to Vega just the echo in her mind of the musein's first call to prayer she heard as Charles came to bed, the call now repeated as the great prayer of the afternoon wound through the city. Yes, she thought, she had been awake a long time, longer than ever before when Charles had come to the flat they shared with Pombal, the French diplomat they had met in Paris. Frailty had never been hers, not when she went without sleep and not when she was forced to endure deprivation and distress. Not that she was a deep well of strength, just that she lived inside more than on the pavement or the bed. Returning from her inward drift, she saw Miss Miller looking at her with a smile that was a question, now voiced: "Are you back now?"

Aware now of her silence, Vega replied: "Just a bit of a drift. I had expected to see you in scarlet and gray, not battle dress." Straightening her blouse, the older woman replied: "Perhaps the gray and scarlet will return but for now and probably forever if this war lasts that long, we will wear khaki slacks and blouses, which I will issue you as soon as you are ready to start. On the day shift, nine to nine, will give you time to get acquainted. And one more thing. That scent you are wearing probably isn't appropriate for the wounded in the wards. It's evocative enough to disturb them. Make them think of other times, which in a way is good. But too much of a distraction can impinge on the healing." Vega smiled inwardly as she remembered some nurses who were more inappropriate in their behavior than wearing something like *Jamais de la vie* that she had found on the handkerchief Charles had dropped in the bathroom. She had tucked it into her pocket. Out of sight and not a topic. She would need to clear her mind of such thoughts and here she could: "You mean to see if I am what I claim to be. I can start tomorrow." With her newly washed slacks and blouse wrapped in brown paper with a little handle of twine, she took the tram away from Sidi Bishr and away from the beach with its elegant homes, where even now those with money could act as if the past gaiety still lived. And for them it did since the Germans had no reason to drop bombs so far from the center of the city. But the tram stopped within walking distance from them to pick up the women who would be called the Marthas back where she had been born, women of the local cast who everywhere cleaned and served in the houses of a largely foreign idle rich minority. That she herself was not of that minority and had shocked her classmates and caused one to say: "Before I met you, I thought Catholics were only maids and gardeners." "Well," said I: "Thank God for the Jew and Irishman who spat in my blood." So much for a social life at Miss Blount's School for Young Ladies in Black Rock and soon passage from dear old dirty Dublin to a less dear and dirtier London that also dripped without regard for the season, causing the inward drift that kept her sane:

"My god, is there no sun in this world. Years later I would long for a bit of gray and rain soaked shoes."

On that first day she saw little and later the more she saw the less she cared, especially when she took the tram back to Alex proper after a twelve hour shift. When she went to bed, Charles would, of course, be up. Often Hamid the servant would have come back from the market and was making coffee. She was still blind to all but the images on her mind's retina of what she had seen in the wards when Miss Miller had shown her where she would work and what to expect, survivors old before their time perhaps soon to be dead before their time when they were "certified" able for service. And the little desk with the death certificates of those who would not return to the desert alive.

But she awoke to Charles' saying: "Bit of a fuss at the office today. A Brigadier by the name of Maskylene seems to think I am a spy."

"A spy? How in the world could he think a clerk could be a spy? That's what you are aren't you? A clerk."

"Well, yes; but I am privy to conversations, to the diplomatic bag, and to the files. And he thinks his own office and its inquiries are being presented to people in the Mission and even to the Foreign Office as the workings of someone trying to elevate his current position to what it had been before the Ambassador moved him to Palestine because of his unrelenting inquiry into the life of Nessim whom he is convinced is the mastermind of an armed Jewish action in Palestine. He even sees Nessim's marriage to a Jewish woman as part of the plot by establishing his bona fides. Also, he thinks I am leaking information about his investigation to the Hosnanis simply because they are my friends." Vega's slight snore was to convince Charles that she had gone back to sleep while he rambled. Not at all true for she lay awake as she had on other nights uttering the soft sounds of sleep listening to his talk mostly as he was sleeping while she tried to blot out his confessions with recollections of their past as a salve for the present: "That little pension in the Plaka just across the street from the Roman Agora was better than this, even with the Germans moving ever closer. There we had each other, ourselves in a quiet bond as our past lives were taken from...." Her thoughts were interrupted by detached phrases Charles mumbled in his sleep: "Nessim outside the dim window casting...while I pulled the sheet...and she pressed against me blocking...us, sheared away like branches dead from a winter storm which left, we hoped, the trunk alive awaiting...." Vega would continue to mock sleep but her eyes stayed open.

The dismal tram ride to the hospital and the living nightmare would not erase what she heard but would at least keep her from replaying this story of deception and lust, carried not only by his ramblings but by the smell of another woman on his skin, his hair, even the way he touched her, the way that woman must have taught him. For he was a man of simple desire, and Vega had never brought the streets of her childhood to their bed. There only the simulacrum of desire earned the hard coin of whatever realm she had been left. To him she gave only the simple loves of her body, no other. By the time she had bathed in the cracked soap stone sink, Hamid had come back from the souk with the only bread there, flat bread baked with rosemary seeds brushed on with olive oil while being toasted on the grill, something the cafe owner Noe brought with him from one of those islands off the coast of Italy. It was served with the thick coffee Hamid knew how to make, not tea which seemed to confuse him. She would leave Charles asleep, and he, for at least twelve hours, would be veiled from her by the blood and cries of pain.

Today she came later, having posted letters and picked up mail. The tram she took was scattered with young people returning home from school. Two sat in front of her, a young boy and girl chatted, comfortably as the young do, though all they had in common was being in secondary schools and not the same one. He wore a blue woolen jacket, she a white muslin blouse, black silk tie, navy blue skirt. She said to the young man next to her: "I am Susu, young man. And who are you?" With a bit of a nervous twitch, he said: "I am called Mikha'l." On hearing that, Susu rose not because her stop was near. Mikha'l was a Coptic name and not one that belonged to someone she might actually be willing to know. Copts and Moslems in her life were as separate as the Marthas and the idle rich of Vega's past. Hopefully, the crestfallen young Copt would not be crushed by a slight he would certainly never forget, though he later would find Moslem women with if not of more egalitarian taste at least ones willing to use and discard him. But for now, he stood on the Cornice before turning to walk the same street Vega did.

Before he could turn, stop looking after Susu, his young sister came running up to him. She said their mother had badly cut herself butchering chickens for feast day. Crying, she said, "You must find help." Stunned and frightened, he started to go to the tram station hoping someone would know of a doctor. No one in his family knew of one. Like all on their street, they relied on the grace of God, until now that is. Vega in her wartime nurse's khaki blouse and baggy trousers, even the children recognized as a nurse. "Please, miss, can you help? Our mother is injured. Badly." Even without an oath that committed her to the care of others, Vega turned and said: "Let us go to your mother." So they went through the half deserted streets, half deserted because only the youngest of the children and the women who did not work were home through the clean streets of the poor. The apartment was on the third floor with the front window towards the sea catching any breeze. The injured woman sat on a plain wooden chair holding her right arm between the blood soaked cloth on her wrist and her elbow. Though frightened when Vega removed the cloth, she did not flinch, her eyes downcast, her body rigid. Never before had she been touched by a foreigner or a medical aid. These people, they took care of themselves, babies delivered by a family member, small illnesses treated as they had always been. But now with only her children at home, she turned outside for help that she felt foolish for needing and chagrined at her own clumsiness as she was about to slaughter the chickens. She had tied them together by their feet so she could throw them over a clothes line with their necks severed bleeding to death without bruising their flesh flapping around on the floor of the terrace. As she raised the knife to the neck of the second chicken the first in its death spasm jolted her hand and she slashed her wrist missing the vein but cutting deeply into muscle. Washing the cut with hot water and a strong soap, Vega wrapped the cut with a clean bandage from the few supplies she had actually picked up earlier. In the manner of those with little money, the mother thanked her and offered fous and fresh bread. A courtesy, Vega accepted and told the boy to change the bandage twice a day and to come to the MMH and ask for Vega if there was any swelling or redness. She left them then, not without some reluctance. These were her own people, not those with whom she now lived, jetsam like her scattered by war to this arid sanctuary.

Though Vega was a bit later than expected, Matron simply welcomed her back from a brief respite. Matron sensed Vega needed. Given a few hours to herself, Vega now sat quietly while Matron briefed her. They had lost several of what those they called their "guests" after the last conflicting surges in the desert that swept away from that little train station. Called what? Yes, that's it—El Alamein. And so Vega had several days that became nights and then days again before she left for Alexandria and the probably empty bed. The merging of the wounded and dead, the merging of day with night, her senses that neither saw, heard nor smelled inured her to who and what she was. She was startled to see the Matron, who sat at her desk with that smile that said, "Welcome back" followed by, "I have a new patient for you, a rather special man who may not leave here. His name is John Keats. He jokingly said that his past was not as a poet but a correspondent. But now he is one of Montgomery's Desert Rats. He heard another nurse,

Diane, I believe, mention your name. And for the first time since he was admitted he responded, saying he thought he had met you with a writer friend of his named Larry Durrell. Even if you don't remember him, a friend now would be good for him. He may well be another of our permanent residents." There was no touch of irony in Matron's voice, only the acceptance of another frequent death as she looked at this young nurse who once again seemed of a kind not often seen among her charges, a foreigner finding a place without war in supposedly neutral Alexandria, someone building a little nest, not just lighting on a lily pad. "So, do you actually know him and if so in a manner appropriate between nurse and patient?" Vega, as she often did, found Matron's manner at odds with her battle dress. But even the gray and scarlet of earlier wars spoke of a propriety belied by writers such as Hemingway, who seemed to have spent his time in hospital thinking that his true vocation would be nurses, not writing. Returning from her troubling thoughts, Vega smiled and said, "Yes, he is an acquaintance more than a friend."

In her timeless and placeless state, she drifted back to before Keats donned khaki. He spent time with Charles, Pursewarden, and Larry Durrell, drones at the British Embassy. John was a correspondent always going to the next place where a story might be about to happen. Now he is of the story. Again she drifted into an earlier knot on the string that was their life and sat, again, with Charles, Larry, Pursewarden, Keats and his friend Aissa in that little cafe on rue Foad. When she arrived, they had been there long enough to be loquacious and amused by the wit and humor the

Green Fairy granted its friends, though not those who chose another path. Being writers freed from that tribe's reluctance to speak of their own writing, they had talked enough to tire Aissa, who simply let her gaze be as blank as what those in the desert called the hundred yard stare.

She was there but only as a body, and having heard several exchanges about the finer points of fine points, Aissa was pleased to see Vega who turned to Larry as he spoke: "If I am ever forced to write of this city and its flora and fauna in order to be rid of you stripped of your disguises, I will have no choice. You will all be not as you appear now but as what she has made of you, what you are when stripped of your disguises, what the spirit of this place, the locus dei, has made you, frail, corrupt, endearing, a bit exotic. Of course, if I am to make any money from such writing. I shall have to make you more interesting, more flawed and more colorful than you are. I shall exercise all license granted an Irish poet and gild you with the juices that will attract all those who live the life of burgers, those who masturbate at night while in bed with their pallid and meaningless others. And above all, I must try to be contemporary so they can feel they no longer inhabit the life they live, those who have never read Marx, and Frazer, and Freud. I must give them dreams." Having assured us that we might not be pilloried, he turned that smile of his, that smile he saved for his mind's eye, towards us, tilted slightly to the left and farted.

Pursewarden, more au domicile with the fairy than were the others, eased around in his chair and replied. "Oh, dear, Larry, how can we thank you for not pulling us along as we are but changing us with your ridiculous fancy as you did with that one armed Irish salt. He became something of a kind when you made him into a hashish ridden bisexual whom you had dubbed the Irish hemiphone. God, you had to stretch language and credibility to make that ancient mariner worth our time. By the way, I looked in several dictionaries for 'hemiphone.' The word doesn't exist. Henry was right when he said you make up words. Miguel, please let the Fairy fly around this table again. Un circle por favor." And turned towards the sea to feel the wind from the right side of the Med.

Larry rose to a riposte: "Ludwig, if I may be so intimate as to call you by your given name, not by the family name draped over you by the father you never knew, all the words I use are real words easily acted to the size of a small nut by being English. Not even British for God's sake."

With the care of one not very steady, Pursewarden placed his glass exactly on the wet circle left by its predecessor and with feigned deference, asked: "Cher maître, to be in the presence of a living dictionary is at once humbling and annoying. I would flounce out of here if I were not unsteady and determined to stay here until I am past unsteady, to stay here until I no longer care what you will do to me if I am interned in one of your cryptic attempts to instruct and delight. I know you will wed me to an ignorant and unhygienic mockery of a wife and load me with an equally distasteful brood in someplace between Hell and Manchester or The Elephant and Castle. You will have fled me to imprisonment dictated by the F.O. and moved me from one arid primitive posting to another, finally settling me in this arid piss pot. What else you have in mind I shudder to imagine. Just pray God, let me kill myself rather be humiliated further by association with such as you." Then tucking his handkerchief in his sleeve, he rose and with the suppport of several chairs wobbled to the gents.

Feigning regret at the interruption, Larry said to those who had long since lost interest:"I have an apt rejoinder that must wait until that lout who cannot limit his output to fewer than three volumes per narrative has extracted himself from the loo." He turned quickly for a small man when his prey returned and said: "Ah, there you are, Ludwig. Well done. You've even buttoned your fly. But before I discuss your inability to dredge up any narrative concern in under seven hundred pages of turgidly boring accounts of sex among the lesser classes dispersed over three volumes with such pretentious titles as *God Created What Man Did Not*, I must ask young Charles here why he seems so utterly bored and inattentive by the pearls we have tossed before him. I can understand that Keats here has nothing to say. Like his namesake he is merely a chronicler of other people's woes and indiscretions. But why you, my dear Charles?"

With newly acquired aplomb, Charles said: "Quite frankly, old dears, I never engage in literary discussions. They are like dogs snuffling around a bitch too small to mount." Lost in thought at this bit of whimsy, Durrell muttered: "Too small to mount" God, I wish I had said that." Turning and almost in a whisper, Pursewarden said: "You will, Larry, you will." Balked into his only possible response, Durrell said: "Oh, aren't you clever to remember that riposte of Whistler."

The table now once again the province of four odd and unmatched men and without an audience other than each other turned to the subject three of them had noticed and one, unfortunately, had not. “Is that stench of *Jamais de la vie* actually coming from one of us?” said Pursewarden as he turned toward Charles. Inattentive until now, Charles bolted upright: “My god, do I really smell of that perfume?” Pursewarden shaking off his guise of alcoholic stupor for he had unheard of capacity said: “As I told you a few weeks ago, if you are going to be bedded by Justine, you must do two things: Leave a change of clothing at the office and talk to that her about anything except what happens in the office.” Shaken, Charles asked: “Is the aroma so strong that Vega would have noticed?”

Turning from the several untouched drinks in front of him, Keats rose from his slump, yawned, and said: “She would have to be dead not to have noticed. Even that half drunk Desert Rat walking down the pavement fumbling for a few coins to buy a tart for half an hour, raised his nose to the scent. Why you would spend time with what Pursewarden in a rare moment of clarity called that ‘old turnstile’ through which we are all expected to pass on our way to Hell. And no I did not drop a penny in the slot. I chose a path much less traveled. Aissa, though she is a part time cabaret dancer and part time whore has just a touch of gravitas left. Her father, you know, was a sergeant in the King’s artillery. Whereas your choice was born in some seedy estiment in a best forgotten city. And yes, Vega knows.” The three men actually looked open mouthed at Keats, the silent chronicler as Larry had called him until finally Larry said: “I am shocked I tell you. Shocked. What has possessed you to speak at this time?” His turn come round at last, Keats spoke: “I’m in for a change in my wardrobe tomorrow and may not be here for some time. I simply wanted to clear my mind before I leave.” “A change of clothes! And a trip? Where could you possibly go to need different clothes and more interesting stories?” This languid dismissal was left to Pursewarden.

Shaking off the comment as a dog does a bit of mud, Keats said: “Khaki and the desert. Tomorrow, I will be not with you but with Monty’s lads. Time to do my bit.”

Larry interrupted the silence by clearing his throat and after rummaging in the inner pocket of his jacket selected a page from the wad of paper. Then read:

> The fixed star of the ancients was another Vega
> A candle burning high in the alps of heaven
> Shielded by rosy fingers on some sill
> Above some darkly sifted lake. They also knew
> The silence trying to perfect itself in words.

The silence of the men was unbroken yet muffled further by the mauve and yellow of the miasma of the setting sun as it closed around the cafe and dimmed those inside to ever distant shadows while she who had left looked out of the small tin tram. Unable to go back to the room she shared with Charles, Vega without thinking went to Sidi Bishr. Without design she stopped at what the locals called the Church of the Two Saints, the Coptic Orthodox

Church of Saint Mark and Saint Peter. Though born into a Catholic family, she was ignorant of all but its rudiments and nothing of the Coptic. Yet feeling a need to be in a place of worship stained by believers, she entered. Finding a pew in the close darkness, she sat, turned and saw she was not alone.

CHAPTER FIVE

Vega was jolted out of the momentary return of her past by Matron saying: "Are you all right, my dear? We seemed to have lost you there for a moment." And said: "I'm fine. I was just recalling the last time I saw Keats. At a gathering with a few friends, he had casually announced he was to change his wardrobe the next day and would be gone for some time, saying in response to the puzzled silence: 'I'll be wearing khaki and stationed in the desert. It's time I did my bit.' He then left the little cafe where my friends were self medicating with the Green Fairy." Matron looked puzzled and said: "Green Fairy?" After explaining more to her than she wished to know, Vega spoke of Keats as a journalist who looked at others instead of himself for a meaning, even for life itself, a man who until recently had shown no interest in a life of his own. "And he has changed. Been brought into this slaughter, this madness, on a whim, perhaps to see firsthand what would be the story that would define this age? If so, he is perhaps doing what writers, especially journalists, have always done, for good and for ill. But to go into battle as a combatant is a leap into the absurd, a contradiction of all he is. Absolutely meaningless."

Again telling Matron much more than she wished to know, Vega mused: "The reason is named Aissa, a part time cabaret dancer and part time whore. Until her, he was like his friends going from faceless lovers to self medication with the Green Fairy and her siblings. Anything to distract, sometimes even to destroy their own sense of worth as they use the war as an excuse for personal debasement, perhaps a desire to destroy what we have created art, literature, culture itself to shield us, protect us from this unrecognized desire to destroy, of which this war, though emblematic, is but a rationale, giving meaning to the reptilian part of us left over from our creation. And no, I do not believe some God looked at this little world and thought to herself: 'Humm, that might be a place where some good can take root.' No intelligent creator would have let that reptile look out through our eyes. Yes, Aissa touched him some way, indescribably, unknown even to himself, though he might call it love. If so, then he mocks his namesake for whom love rode with lovers only to destroy them."

As an easy dismissal of Vega's disturbing meditation, Matron said: "I minister to the religious and tend the wounded, neither of whom have purchase in the realm you seem to know so well. If it exists, I can do nothing for those who inhabit it. Keats is but a few aisles away and has asked to see you. Come. I'll take you to him." And so they walked through the ward closest to the exit, closest to the battles, to the desert where the almost ambulatory, those who without a touch of irony are called "the walking wounded." Hidden away from the outside world were those lacking limbs and those who in their dreams called "Mother" or "medic." The walk was brief before Matron opened a door to a room with windows looking out past the palm trees towards the sea where even now svelte young people swam as if no war existed. Keats's bed was placed so that he could look out that window, smell the sea carried on the wind, and perhaps see in his memory's eye the svelte young. Vega moved so that he could see her yet not lose the view. "Keats, I haven't seen you since that absinthe outing you had with the remnants of the British Mission, when the Green Fairy eased the war into a daze and you told of your change in wardrobe. I regret your change of place was so brief. Is there anything I can do?" He turned his head on the pillow slightly towards her and with scant irony said: "To take the items in order. Morphine tells even sweeter lies than absinthe. At times I actually think I will leave here, even though I won't. Then, as long as what I think of as the Blue Fairy has her grip on me, my namesake's lady stays in the fog. What I need you to do is ask Pursewarden and Larry to visit me, quite soon actually. Then you might check to see if the Blue Fairy is just waiting at the door."

Vega's day, as were they all, was long and this one, again, ministered to by the aroma of *Jamais ma vie*, a ministry that no longer troubled her self. A place of peace in a distant land was hers, and there she was not alone. She was part of the meaning that underlay the human experiment. Such matters were actually experienced without reflection yet guided her existential self. But now that self was to lie quiet, perhaps dormant, as she left Keats to attend those who would survive to return to the front or to a way station on their way to Blighty. The hours she was there had no definition but were a simple continuum that ended sharply when someone tapped her on the shoulder and said, "Off you go." And go she did, following the course that was no longer thought about but was like a ritual she followed without thinking as some people cross themselves when passing a church or a cemetery. Without thought or intent, she left for the dismal outskirts of the city, then to the city herself. Alex to the Brits who so despised this city arid and on the wrong side of the Med who gave it this familiar dismissive name, thus making it theirs and not the city whose real spirit was to be found in the bones of those who made this place redolent, the Boy King who gave it his name, the great queen and her Anthony who gave all for love. None of this mattered to her then or ever. Lost as she was to time she woke only when she entered the flat she shared with Pombal and Charles.

There they all sat with the dinner brought back from Naafa, bully beef, canned milk, English tea, and canned peaches. Seating herself at the table she declined the bully beef, accepted a mug of Navy tea, regular tea strengthened with condensed milk and sugar until it was almost soup, nourishing but foul. Turning to Larry and Pursewarden, whom she could not call Ludwig, she told them all they would want to hear of her day, and even that or perhaps especially that would cause a ripple of uneasy silence in these men for whom the war was not her visceral one: "Our friend John Keats is now under my care but not for long. He has asked to see you, Larry, and you, Pursewarden. As I hope you understand, his stay though brief will also end with us. He wishes to see you not together but separately and soon. He knows he is dying. We did chat awhile about the past. But perhaps that is best left as undocumented history, much like Alexander's lovers."

The next morning when Vega, washed and dressed in khaki, went to the shared room of the flat for coffee and some flat bread, Larry was there, relaxed but expectant: "Alright if I go with you today? Best to see Keats early from what you said." Glancing up, Vega murmured: "Of course, the tram leaves within the hour." Neither the tram ride nor their entering the hospital changed the quiet, reflective mood of Durrell. He seemed to be gathering himself as he had when he and Nancy, with daughter in tow, left Corfu as the Germans moved south. But this time the war had come to him as a man he had never treated with other than the mild indifference he always showed for mere onlookers, those who create nothing, not a painting, not a poem. Now facing the reversal of roles, he recalled some of Keats's reflections on men of action and those who created, wondering which was directed to serve the greater good. He had little time to wonder before Vega took him to the room.

Keats looked up as Durrell entered and said: "I am reminded now of a time in Madrid at the Hotel Florida. The walls were shaking from the fascist's bombardment. We hunkered to avoid the blast as the wall disappeared. When I turned to speak to Juan, he was dead. A few days later I left for London. I was helping to ferry ambulances." Moved, almost charitably, Durrell said: "You were in Spain during the Civil War? I did not know that." Keats's response was that of a man who held a hidden card: "Ah, laddy buck, I have pieces of my life, bits of information tucked away that I never so much as talk about, much less write about. Such as your affair with the French Cardinal's mistress." So shocked Durrell sat bolt upright and exclaimed: "What!" Keats's wry smile held as he continued: "Surely you remember when Cardinal Marin came to Alexandria to strengthen the spiritual life of his French community. You seemed to have known Jacqui and struck up a rather close association with her, so close that the Cardinal said he and you could never again be friends unless you confessed your sins. Your reply, though apt, probably ended a perfectly good friendship. 'Your Eminence, I regret having pulled from under you, so to speak, the woman with whom you were committing adultery and breaking your vow of celibacy.'" Even Durrell's sang froid fell as he chuckled: "That's a lie! And besides, her name was Lisette." Waving aside a possible return to this episode of their past, Keats said: "During that absinthe outing at the Cafe Pierre, you said you would have to make us more interesting if you ever wrote about our time here. Have you actually considered such and what would you do? I have some interest in my future in print, especially since I have left only a brief one in fact."

With marked relief, Larry said: "For some time, I have gathered material, notes about places, scraps of dialogue, and sketches of people for what I have, as a working title, called *The Book of the Dead*, the title obviously derived from *The Egyptian Book of the Dead*. I have, in general, taken who we all are and gathered us into a close, even somewhat incestuous, group that exploits what I call modern love, a condition free of periodicity, affection, even lust, yet subject to the intrusion of any of these." Such conversations, Keats usually ignored but feigned interest in ones that might defile him: "Good god, without these, what is left to encourage even casual sex. Even in a swamp of dissolution such as this." Larry, though, as always, attuned to his own thoughts, said: "You overlook the adjective 'modern.' Modern man, woman as well, have the weight of the ages substituting appearance for desire in an exhausted psyche, a psyche seeking meaning even if that meaning is only that a purpose for the human animal directs its thoughts even when those thoughts have as their only reason to be is to extract from both individuals and groups an identity that can be substituted for traditional love. The troubadours died a long time ago. I will portray you much as you were since I find this incarnation beyond my vision. Perhaps later. Pursewarden will remain. And I will pillory that arrogant sod. Robertson must go and be replaced by a seedy English minor and threadbare academic. This is a story about Brits with no room for Colonials. Nessim and Justine will be central to this tale of modern love. He without sex and she without passion. I have yet to find, or to accept, an idea to bring coherence to this unlikely crew other than the war which really only functions to bring them to Alexandria after they have exhausted all other residence. So there you have it. Sorry I couldn't do more with you, but actually you didn't give me much to work with being outside my concept of modern love. Aissa for whom you have a disturbingly real affection, even love for, makes you an anomaly. You will have to be a cipher. Sorry."

Accepting with what grace he had, Keats gave a final broadside: "I expect though Aissa should and could continue even morph into someone who matters. But you have ignored others. Yourself for one. And Nancy who took your daughter when she left you and went to Palestine. Oh, and Nancy, by the way, is living with Mike Silver. And then there is the time the three of you spent on Corfu which covers you like the golden shafts of sunlight coming through the olive trees reflecting off the wine dark sea, blah, blah. And gives me a lukewarm smile because you still want to love in that high old fashion. But enough for now. My friend the Fairy is bidding me to drift into the cool mountains and bathe in the pure streams. Or so I fancy."

At the door, Larry stopped and saw the pale knight and wondered how long before she took him away, not to return. As he looked down the aisle, away from the front door, he saw Vega, though she did not see him. Her full attention was on a man still on the stretcher. As the soldiers who had borne in their comrade passed him, one said: "You a doctor?" and he replied: "No, just an observer." And walked out of the bedlam (in the old sense of the word) of the nearly silent wards into the late October mild warmth that had brought not long ago the Mission from Cairo to spend the winter in Alexandria. His reflections on the social season that would try to ignore the search lights, the bombs were interrupted by a greeting, and looking up he saw Pursewarden. The two men stopped on the walkway with the hospital looming behind them and the promised escape of the sea in front of them, Durrell said: "Going to see Keats. If so, don't dawdle. His time is narrow, and his path blurred by what he calls the Blue Fairy. Morphine. You will need relief when you leave. The Pierre."

As had Durrell, Pursewarden cringed inwardly as the real war came to him, not alive but wounded and dying in the hollowed and scarred faces, the broken bodies, the voices caught in mid scream that were ministered to by khaki clad women. He had seen the old photos from the war to end all wars: women clad in gray and scarlet hovering over men in wheel chairs or posing on their crutches with grins on faces too young to be there. He paused, blinked and saw for the first time that those photographs were as posed as those Brassaï took in Montparnasse. These men would not be photographed unless they were tidied up. Reflecting on life and art, he met Vega. She led him down the hall to a room. He entered and saw Keats, propped up in bed and looking out his window at the sea breeze rattling the palms. He stopped inside the door and watched for a moment until Keats, sensing his presence, turned and said: "Don't stand upon ceremony. Come, sit, and I will settle a pillow by my head tell you all." Pursewarden disguised his queasy mind with a pedantic quip: "If you are going to quote Eliot, even from that wretched "Prufrock," at least get it right. But then you may actually have improved it." Tapping his pocket, he said: "A touch of The Fairy?"

Still looking out his window, Keats in a class defining drawl said: "Not now or ever again. I have left her for another love, one who comes to me rather than my going to her. Right now, I am between dream and pain. A good time for me to show you why I have asked you to visit me, other than for the always rare delight of your company. You can ask me anything about what I give you except where I got it. You will understand my reserve when you read it. Open the drawer in the table beside my bed and take out the green small octavo." Doing as Keats asked, Pursewarden took the book from the drawer, opened it and read the list of names on the inside cover. The first was Nessim Hosnani, then Leila Hosnani, then Balthazar, followed by some Coptic and Jewish names, and a few French and German, names he did not know. Inscribed above them was the name Joshua Cohen. Glancing through the book, he saw lists of names associated with times and places, what appeared to be bills of lading, weaponry and munitions listed by name and quantity, places of delivery and recipients. Bemused, Pursewarden asked: "Just what am I looking at?" Still with his eyes averted, Keats almost *sotto voce* said: "This is documentation that illustrates how Nessim organized and directed a plot to arm Jewish guerrillas in Palestine. His mother was the mind behind this effort, and Balthazar's Cabal and its wide correspondence was the means by which all the Copts listed stayed in touch. The Germans were representatives of Krupp; the French names were their bankers. They are rightly assured that Egypt will have a Moslem government not welcoming to Copts when the Brits leave. Knowing that the Jews will establish their long desired homeland and become the power brokers of this whole area, they meant to or hoped to bribe the Jews to protect them. The idea is, of course, insane. The Jews don't give a fuck for the Copts, and the Moslems will bleed them of everything they have in and out of Egypt. And, by the way, Maskylene knows some of this and soon may know enough to string Nessim up by any part of his body he chooses."

Sitting in stunned silence, Pursewarden was speechless and said after a significant but long and awkward pause: "Two questions: how sure of all this are you and why me rather than say Durrell or even Ambassador Mountolive?" Keats waiting for his final breath, whispered: "If you wish validation, wait for Maskylene to act. He will soon and force the Ambassador to do something. Both Mountolive and Durrell are close to the Hosnanis and will sooner or later be caught in the net. If I gave this wee book to either of them, they might think that informing Nessim is the only way to proceed and so save their friend and keep egg off the face of the Empire. So you see, though you thought I was just peeping over transoms and looking under beds, I was actually following those who were under the beds—and in them, no, not for the seamy little stories of marital infidelities of which there were many and varied. The cast of players had no sane narrative coherence. What could have brought these people together, not money or sex or even sexual desires? What could possibly draw a renowned sexual artist, though a tawdry one, such a Justine to a clumsy novice like Robertson? And why would Nessim allow it? Or why did our monkish friend marry her?" Pursewarden, mouth actually open and eyes twitching, gestured toward Keats with a bottle before having a long draw himself. Brushing aside the absinthe with a smile, Keats said, "I have my own frequent visitor, brought to me by the peerless Vega," who entered the room and with a gesture that told Pursewarden to wait outside.

In a few minutes, she showed him to a small room next to a storage area for bed linens. Looking at him not with scorn but with little interest, she said: “I want to tell you how Keats ended up here and a bit about that journal you’re hiding. Yes, I know what it contains, and I have no interest in the dalliances, no matter how monumental, of such a self serving bunch of ciphers as you and your friends. You will, as do onlookers, continue to serve the state or what other abstractions occupy your interest, while Keats and those like him disappear from the world and probably disappear from your memory. ‘My bit’ as he called putting himself in harm’s way was to serve in Monty’s 239 Anti-tank Battery. They needed replacements after their Phyric victory at Snipe left them with one gun and depleted ranks. At one time, I wondered what the lot of you would do when this carnage ends. I no longer care, and when I can, I will go where life makes sense. Since Larry is obviously waiting, you should go.”

And so he did. Riding the dismal little tin tram back to the city, back to the cafe where Larry was nursing nothing stronger than a glass of red wine. Lost in thought, he was startled as Pursewarden sat down heavily across from him and gestured to the waiter for one of the same: “I assume you are as empty and chagrined as I, wondering what we are to do and have done.” Taking the small green book from his jacket pocket and placing it between them on the table, he said: “I read this on the tram coming here. After you have read it, we must decide what to do, for duty and friendship will be in conflict.” Pursewarden sat back and looked away as Larry picked up the book, opened it, and saw the list of names. Rifling through the pages, he saw the lists, the narratives, the time line, and said: "Where the hell did you get this!" More troubled than ever by himself, Pursewarden said: "From Keats who refused to say anything about how he came by it or its origin except that it is the personal record of Joshua Cohen. He knows he is dying and has left us with the responsibility of deciding what do with it since he is relieved of whatever intent he may have had. The grave's a fine and quiet place, but none I think there do betray their friends nor do their duty to God, King, and Mammon. I assume from your silence you are as stunned as I by the documented actions of friend Nessim." Reflective, but not dismissive, Larry replied: "No. I have heard rumbles or rather overheard rattlings. Maskylene has been to see David about rumors his network has picked up about a Jewish group in Palestine that is receiving funding from some source in Egypt. He suspects the Copts but only suspects. Obviously, this journal has to go to David. The question for us is: do we tell Nessim? If we don't, he will be destroyed. And if we do...." And so he ignored the wine placed in front of him.

Pursewarden did what writers do more often in times of stress and distress than in times of pleasure or even simple contentment. He turned to writing, on this occasion not his but his companion's: "We need, I think, to call up the past, a wee distraction from the present to let this settle and gain some sense of the thing. I've been bemused somewhat that when you talk of your writing now, you never mention Corfu and all that. Do you just not want to revisit your soon to be ex-wife?" Quirked more than he showed, Durrell, simply said: "Not at all. And what do you know about my marriage?" Assuming his customary airiness, Pursewarden replied in kind: "Just what we have all heard. That she left you when you threw yourself with much enthusiasm and little discretion into the sea of women in which we all swim in this most compatible sea of excess." The distraction succeeded, and Durrell rose to the bait: "If I can ever find a way to be rid of you and your intrusive, bourgeois, tacky, smug, messing about, I will do so even if I have to kill you, No. Better yet. I will have that sister of yours marry and leave you to whatever you chose in your smug celibacy. And if you must know, I have 20,000 words on that time in Corfu. Though I do not mention her by name, she is present and identified as N." With the upper hand, so different from the one ascribed to Larry, Pursewarden replied: "Softly, dear boy, softly. You will not be able to exorcise that time so easily, as I well know. My current novel in progress, at a splendid 35,00 words if you please, does address that forbidden topic. Not directly of course but by way of a dream about Arsionoe. And for good measure, lurking in the background is a sturdy beef to the heels chattel, to steal from old Dublin Jimmy, of a fishwife who bears a startling resemblance to my own dear wife in that semi-detached horror in Tunbridge Wells. She could have lived in St. James Park but oh no, not with all those toffs putting on airs and farting through silk, plain cotton knickers not good enough for them and teaching my own little brats not to hold the pinky out from the tea cup, just too common. Too uppity by half."

Still with the trace of a grimace, Larry looked and said: "My time will come, Ludwig you ass, when I put all to rights, bring to life and print *The Book of the Dead*. Be assured you will be there in your tattered glory, and Nancy will not be there. But my daughter will be there, more alive than the rest of you and may God strike me down if this is not so. She will share in my own Eden, a much better one than the Great Jew in the Sky created because I gave a new life to it not being content with Paradise enow to paraphrase the old poet. Now let us drink a bit of this red wine, share a bit of what the cafe has to offer in the way of food. Then, perhaps tomorrow, make a decision about this troubling, hopefully, fanciful journal." Unwilling to leave a winning hand, Pursewarden spoke over the glass: "I accept all, except fanciful. You must fight your tendency to clutter up your discourse with adjectives and adverbs, Mere barbarisms."

The next day was cool, even for winter in Alexandria, and the meeting between the two confidants was neither cordial nor unpleasant. It teemed with necessity, with that which was unwelcome, unavoidable and moving them inevitably to the office of Sir David Mountolive, whom heretofore they had always called David, or your Ex. But now on entering, he was Sir David to Larry and Mr. Ambassador to Pursewarden as the two stood before his desk, not hangdog but a bit chagrined and not accepting the proffered chairs, instead standing like schoolboys caught snugging in the loo and expecting a whack on the exposed backside.

Elegant in his civil tonsure, Sir David looked at them with a bit of puzzlement and said: "Although I am pleased that you have at last seen fit to recognize, perhaps even respect, the necessity of your being somewhat servile, I do wonder what has caused this sudden change. Unless, of course, irony or even a smile has prompted you." Saying only, "Please look at this" as he placed the green bound journal on the desk between them, stepping back to stand beside Pursewarden, Durrell waited, then said, "Some of this, but only some, has been in Maskylene's reports, such reports as caused you to transfer his office to Jerusalem. Some other action by you, if not in response to the Brig, will probably be necessitated," and then with a sigh and a small smile he said: "Probably putting Nessim in the soup." Looking up from the first page, Mountolive with his head to one side and more than pensive dismissed the two with a small gesture, saying only, "Later." By the time they opened his door, he was talking on his phone. By the time they were in the hall, closing the door behind them, people were coming out of their offices. They moved in a vortex with the center being the office of Mountolive. When Durrell and Pursewarden reached their office, they were no longer relevant. The swirling parts had settled.

Justine and Charles no longer entwined rejoined what Justine had endured of his caresses and spoke softly to him: "Everything you told me went into the dispatch box, Cohen's journal, Maskylene's notes, and Mountolive's suggested alternatives for actions?" Behind the soft voice was a hiss the kitten would have known presaged a barely smothered desire to crush its skull. Soon, he might well wish he had gone to the desert with Keats. There at least was purpose, though with death. What he faced was life without purpose, without this lover who dressed and left him without a word or glance. Pombal's flat was empty, devoid of sound and devoid of any sign of Vega. She left no note, and as had Justine, she left not even a scent. He sat and looked out the window at the sun baked street with a breeze rattling the palms.

The journal that should have been a bomb shattering all political and social policies and practices in the Embassy immediately upon its being placed on Mountolive's desk did not. Instead torpor like quiet settled, and all moved about as in a fog, not touching each other and rarely speaking. All waited for the flurry of telegrams and messages between Alexandria and London to coalesce into some action. For some any action was better than feeling as they did, like flies caught in amber, looking alive but dead. Weeks passed after the original of the journal had been sent in the diplomatic box to London, sent after Charles had made the duplicate. He had found a new place in the building, moved away from Durrell and Pursewarden, who had been sent to Coventry for being bearers not only of bad news but of any news. Politics functions best when it functions not at all, when good news goes up and a pat on the head or a touch of the whip goes down. But now, something had to be done, and everyone knew that. Stasis was the nervous life of the Mission. Most stayed in their accustomed offices and continued with their daily and weekly tasks, none too tasking. Some, such as Charles Robertson, were moved closer to the center of the vortex and stayed there after all movement ceased. And there were Durrell and Pursewarden, sitting quietly in their room, spoken to by none and speaking only to each other. They could not have chosen a more satisfying life for themselves. No longer did they erect the semblance of activity, sending menials scurrying with messages, frowning over news releases that were never released, scheduling nonexistent meetings. Now they did what they had done before behind veils that would have been the envy of Salome. They wrote. And Durrell on *The Book of The Dead.* And Pursewarden wrote on one of those multi voluminous works of fiction about the fictional lives of the English when they are not at home. Frequently, that is daily, they left their one remaining minion with some time consuming and meaningless task and went to lunch, a long comfortable lunch, over which they broke the rule all writers live by: If you are going to write, write, don't talk. Especially not to another writer for that writer will resent what is good and delight in exposing any fault.

"So, Ludwig, what has happened to that incestuous and sexually indiscriminate quartet you deposited in the south of France. There to assuage guilt with continued excess?"

With no surprise or even interest, Pursewarden replied: "I readily accept that they are incestuous, or at least two are. But they are not sexually indiscriminate. They are multi-sexual moving in the eternal roundel set in motion when the moving spirit set the threesome at play in what some call Eden. I believe you actually accept the possibility of such a place, having referred to your threesome on Corfu as such." Badgering the moot, Durrell continued: "To treat your disquisition with more respect than it deserves, let me begin: multi-sexual is not a word because no sexual act, if limited to a single species, can be other than bi-sexual." The "Poopoo" comment by Pursewarden did not deter Durrell, who continued: "Accepting Eden as other than an analogy, and relying on all known texts, only two, one male and one female, were in Eden. And my threesome in Corfu, as you termed it, was that of the core family, the building block of civilization: husband, wife, and offspring." While the smile on Pursewarden's face did not offer an acceptable response, it did annoy Durrell enough that he raised his eyebrows and said: "Well?" And left the field to his companion's reply: "Your bona fides as a man of the dictionary are non-existent. Remember the Irish hemiphone? Not even the OED secreted away in the Ambassador's library accepts the existence of Gnostic texts on which your manuscript relies, especially those of the pessimistic inclination. These you will not find in the upstairs library tucked away between the OED and Ovid. But you will find them hidden away among Balthazar's herbs, mystical bric-a-brac, and arcane manuscripts. Because you amuse him, you can be reasonably assured he will show you them. Especially if you bring him a treat, such as that nice boy who brings the Ambassador his elevenses."

Rising in feigned fury, Durrell said: "You insufferable prig. I will not credit anything you have written or said nor will I follow your reasoning or your making diverse views of a single reality copulate without cause into a multi-volume monument to sexuality. I resent your making the Taj Mahal out of something as simple as a toss among the unwashed. You need your head and your genitalia properly screwed on. Yes, I chose screwed with its alternate meaning in mind. Though I doubt you are mature enough for *Tropic of Cancer,* I will loan you my copy, which I fished out of a urinal in Corfu, probably tossed there by an American tourist on his way home from Paris. Or perhaps by a middle class Englishman who did the toss after intoning, 'This just isn't quite right, doing dirt on life this way.' What Henry and I are writing will put what you and those like you where you belong, with the curiosities of literature, with Rider Haggard, with Madame Blavatsky, perhaps even with Bridges's rewrite Hopkins' poems. *The Book Of the Dead* will finally come into being as a single resounding and mature view of contemporary life, love, and lust." As they thrust and parry in the old style, the plot that had granted them leave finally found a resolution from London.

The Ambassador in petulant discomfort had waited for London to make a decision, and finally they had. Neither the Crown nor any of its surrogates would act. Instead, he, Sir David, would deliver to the appropriate office of the Egyptian government a highly redacted summary of Cohen's journal. Redacted meant: no bills of lading, no matters of bank drafts, no contracts, no specific dates, and above all only one name: Hosnani. Only the family name to be mentioned. And the text was to be formally delivered with all proper expediency by the Ambassador himself. Reading the letter, now decoded by Errol, Mountolive recalled advice given him by his former, and last, Head of Mission: "Never act in support of a minority opinion, and never assume you can act independently." And in recalling these dictates, he thought, "I as well as any can be thrown to the wolves in the name of what is for the good of the Service."

As Mountolive sat in his office looking out over the green lawn steadily darkening in the twilight, he lit the thin cigar he favored and took a sip of the whiskey, liking its smoky taste and the familiar heavy comfort of the Waterford tumbler. As he sat, the thought he had been avoiding found form: "This is the end of something. And I really don't know what the the is or what the something is. Hell, I don't even know what the end is. But it all will become if not clear at least evident tomorrow when I see the Egyptian Minister of the Interior and reveal to him what he, assuredly, already knows; for his informants among us are at least as good as ours among them."

In the late morning, after coffee and toast, he stood in his underwear talking with the all too deferential Erroll, secretary without comparison, about what to wear.

"I think coat and tails?" All knowing yet deferential, the secretary agreed: "The Gypos respond best to ceremonial dress. Perhaps, the formal Ambassador's dress would be appropriate to the occasion. Remember how impressed they all were when you arrived wearing it. And it is a perfect fit." Letting details conceal concern, Mountolive replied: "Really, the Tiger Tim weighs at least fifty pounds with all that gold frogging on that heavy blue jacket and trousers. And then the cock hat with the ostrich feathers, not to mention that the sword is bent. Really, I should have paid Sir Louis a great deal less because of that sword. God, I didn't know how good I had it in Russia. But if you really think so, get the thing out while I make a note or two for cues. I've decided to edit even further London's brief. I'll not mention the name Hosnani at all. Just say an Egyptian source. And no mention of actually arming the Jews. Just support for the expected state and homeland for Jewry. What do you think?" Slipping into the trousers Elliot held for him and fastening the braces so they didn't chafe his shoulders, he reflected: "I should to appease London at least indicate the station of the Egyptian source, perhaps say a wealthy Copt. What?" "At least that," said Errol as he held the jacket for Mountolive to put his arms into. Moving his shoulders slightly to settle the jacket, Mountolive mused: "No, friendship aside, I will mention Hosnani but not actually name Nessim. London will not accept less." Storing this tidbit, Errol replied: "A wise decision, sir. And will you mention the Jewish group by name?" Standing quite still while Errol buttoned the jacket, Mountolive spoke with his chin raised and his voice quite ambassadorial: "Of course." Fitting the bent sword into its scabbard and settling the cock hat on his head, looking at his most splendid self in the pier glass, he said: "And London."

"Quite right, Sir David. The car is outside." And so the newly minted and chagrined representative of the Empire left his chambers, then the Embassy itself, and entered the Rolls, its door held open with great deference by the always deferential Errol, who would go far in the Service.

CHAPTER SIX

Vega sat in the Church of the Two Saints in her accustomed pew in a deeply shadowed corner. She came there often, coming there now only from the detritus of war, the torn bodies, the shattered minds behind the eyes that stared blankly or furtively holding quiet the mouths that would only utter sounds at night when they called for the consolation of the past or for the ending of pain in the present, calls of Mother and Medic, sometimes but not often for God. Even in extremis, they knew that if God cared enough to help, God hadn't cared enough to keep them from here. At one time, she had come here leaving behind another form of detritus, that of her steadily emptying life with Charles. But she came not as an escape but as a memory of the consolation and comfort that belief had given to the many or, at least, to a few. Here in this room that smelled of emptiness and devotion, a path had been thought into being, and often followed, between the pleasure and pain of mortality and the absence of both in the martyr's triumph. The absence of the person now gone from their life left them with a mild state of emptiness, which probably directed their way to each other. But to see each other in the Church did not offer such secular discourse as they needed.

And so as they had sat together at Pastroudi's. There they had first talked when they were part of a couple. Now they talked to divest themselves of the under life of their emptiness, probably more of an absence than an emptiness. Neither actually felt a loss and so talked about their lives with the others to conceal not reveal. For between the inner sign and the word is a veil or shadow though not impermeable yet not transparent.

Turning to Nessim in the quiet of the church, Vega observed: "You no longer have the car." And Nessim, without looking at her or even turning his head, replied: "It was the first to go when I had to buy freedom and life. Life for me, but not for my brother." Even Vega was not so inured by daily death that she could keep the shock from her voice: "Narous is dead?" And again Nessim without affect or even a change in voice concurred: "He is dead, a sacrifice demanded and acquiesced to by me to save our mother, myself, and our associates who hoped to provide a place for Coptic Egypt between the powers to be, the Moslems and the Jews." But in his heart, Nessim was keening as much as he could, remembering all. Perhaps he sought solace as he retreated into what he could not utter: "Behind the veil I found images inescapably forced on me. My brother, our father's gun dog sitting by the old man's knee looking at him with the twisted grin left on his face by the badly treated cleft palate, looking and waiting, his great whip curled on the knee of his Turkish trousers stained with sweat and smelling of horse. In the desert, his body shredded by bullets, the great whip curled on the pommel of the saddle of the horse that stood waiting for him. Above the image desert birds circled. By the image only I stood. His servants had not been with him nor at the house."

Nessim was brought back to what he could expect by Vega's voice: "But why? A desert lord. A farmer. He had nothing to do with your plot to save the Copts." For the first, only, time, Nessim's voice was inflected with concern: "You knew of all this?" She spoke as if from a distance: "Yes, Keats had talked with Cohen before he died and was given his journal. Troubled by the sensitivity of the revelations, he had me read it before he gave it to Pursewarden, instructing him to see that it was given to Mountolive. You were mentioned by name. Someone, obviously, saw a need to protect you. That little book could have compromised a great many, not just Copts."

Vega then sat back in her chair, moving her head slightly to be in shadow and let Nessim's stare go unremarked. But the sign itself was her all, mountain ranges topped with snow and wispy clouds, faint sounds of bells, forests with other natural sounds of birds she had never before heard, prophetic not dreamlike. And she knew she must soon leave here as would Nessim who sat in front of her, also lost in a moment. Though he shook his head and said to her: "I feel that I can tell you all, not simply because you already know what the journal contained but because you and I share an experience." Without even concern, much less the distain she could justify, she simply recited: "If you mean Charles and Justine, there is nothing there to share. She behaved in your interests, and he was a willingly duped fool. What we share, to use your word, is our awareness. We know the other life. What I know of it is what was left to me when all else was taken, when this body was tattered because I was materially poor and abandoned. But you came to this other life while you lived with power, privilege. None of this you seemed to have valued until you made an incomprehensible marriage to a sexual doormat over which you all must pass. Pass into what, I ask you. He and the others were already meaningless profligates up to their ears, as Larry said, in the sexual provender of Alexandria, a place made even more empty of emotional and physical value by this War, as do all wars which take and do not give. How wrong Hemingway was to espouse a creed of dying with grace. People simply die and whatever they were goes away, usually not to a better place." The name familiar to Nessim from the remembered sanctity of his study, made Nessim for the nonce a man with a life protected: "Hemingway? You have read Hemingway?" Not sharing Nessim's retreat into the distraction of a literary chat, she said: "Very little and none I value. I knew him in Madrid. He was there. Death with grace is simply the self aggrandizement of a frightened man and is of no relevance here. You lived with power and wealth, though you might as well have been a monk with a begging bowl. Then, for reasons I cannot fathom, you coupled with the Whore of Babylon."

Resurrecting his once accustomed *amour proper*, Nessim said: "I did not 'couple' with her as you clearly meant. She was offered up to me as a useful agent in my dealing with the Jews. What better way to establish my bona fides with them, or so Balthazar said. In the merger, I gave all that I am and have and will have in this union with a divorced Jewess of well established profligacy. I know now that I was silly, both to 'couple' with Justine and to ally myself with Balthazar for whom destiny was greater than friendships. But to explain, not defend, myself, I knew little of the world of physical passion and the blood ties of religion. I was a secular Copt without desire to be sexual in any way." So saying, he sat back for another moment lost to his surroundings, slightly aware that he was with someone and reflected or mused: "Thinking I must have some kind of physical ailment or injury I could not remember, I saw a variety of doctors. All said that I was sound, physically, and could offer no other recourse. Finally, I met with a doctor at the French Embassy who examined me and agreed with the assessment. Then he said, 'Well, if the body is healthy and ready for love, then you must not want to. N'est pas?' Finding this statement incomprehensible, I looked at him and thought only a Frenchman would think that if one could make love and did not, he must be insane. And I said as much. To which he replied: 'No, no, chere aime, doctors far better than I have surmised that working without our awareness are forces within us, these I do not understand, not physical forces, that can act, even control, our behavior. When you told me why you were late today, I knew I could do nothing for you. To be struck dumb on a tram by the flowery cologne of a school girl speaks of something about which neither of us can understand.' He gave me the name of one such doctor, in Zurich. After a few months of embarrassment, I went to see him." Vega had sat quietly through his muttering, but now looked at him and said: "You went to see Jung?" Bewildered Nessim said: "Yes. But how you did know I meant Jung? So few people I know have even heard of him." Vega said: "I talked with him years ago, and we still keep in touch. We share an interest in what you call the occult and what we think of as the spiritual. And so your denied or repressed sexuality will continue?" With a shrug redolent of a Frenchman, he said: "So it seems. I became aware of the process, to speak clinically, that caused my ah condition. As Jung said, 'What is repressed in the conscious life will emerge in the unconscious.' Though he does not, as you probably know, adhere to Freud's theory of childhood sexuality, in my case he thought something had happened to me that I repressed and so it had taken up residence in my unconscious, in the shadow actually. There in that repository of primitive and disturbing presences is my dirty little secret." So said Vega: "None of the joys of intimacy with another or seeing the future of yourself in an offspring will ever be part of who you are?" Without affect, Nessim replied: "No. After my visit with Jung by chance I met a woman whose presence, calm in body and spirit, was such that we did become lovers, briefly, companions, forever. Aissa and I have a child, a daughter. They are no longer in Egypt and are safe from all violence." As he spoke, Vega looked at him without blinking and with understanding but could not resist a quip: "So even with only one eye, you see all the more clearly?" With the semblance of a smile Nessim replied: "Yes, as you say, during that air raid, at last, I am able to be part of a life that has meaning beyond or instead of my life that was blinded by phantasmagoria. Even though I lost the eye when patrolling the inner city as an air raid warden, I found a sense of meaning in life. I was part of life, not just an observer. If I can be of help to you, ask me now. One day, hopefully soon, I will not even be a source of profit for some and a source of smug rejection for others." As Nessim turned to leave, he was surprised to see that Vega seemed not to have noticed his leaving nor had she gone inside herself, as the saying is. Instead, she had seen all and accepted all. She knew at this point what she had left of this place.

Vega had found Alexandria by necessity not by choice. The war dislocated so many and scattered them around the globe, changing lives forever, though she was not one of those so changed as the Matron often thought to herself. And now, seeing Vega sitting in her small space in the nurses' quarters, she decided to speak with her, not about her life or her work but about the books on the small shelf beside her bed, books she had noticed, one in Chinese, one in French, and one in English. As Matron noticed, Vega traveled lightly, few clothes as well as few books, a skirt, a change of trousers, another pair of shoes, and a few underclothes. Possessions did not burden her. Seeing that Vega was holding the book in Chinese, Matron asked, "How in the world did you come to learn Chinese?" Vega's quiet recital of old thoughts surprised Matron into actually listening to what Vega said: "After the death of my mother and the departure of my father, I made my life on the street, in any way I could and soon came to understand that my physical life was of a different order from my spirit. But I was untutored and substituted distraction for thought and meditation. I could be apart from what my body did or needed to do. Though I knew nothing of meditation, I was living a semblance of it. Then I was taken into the family, of sorts, of a wealthy Chinese merchant. I was with him in China until he found my absorption into the ways of a holy man made me of scant value to him. So he left me there, with the parting gesture of enough money to keep me there, he thought, until I needed him again. I did not, though, need either his money or him, for the holy man took me to one of the places of the Dao. There I stayed for two years, until the approach of the war necessitated even those of peace if also European to leave. So I went as I believe I was directed to where I was needed and found a place here."

In this unaccustomed time and place, both lacking death as purpose, Matron wondered about her fellow nurse and said: "Perhaps because I am C of E and of an age that knows little outside my upbringing, I admit to never having heard of the Dao. Is that the term?" And Vega also in this newly formed bubble, said: "Dao or Tao is an ancient Chinese way of understanding the self and the universe, with attention given also to ones society. The teachings are to help one align with the forces of nature and the universe, to be part of the nature of things that are eternal and not to struggle against them for either personal gain, either material or spiritual. You may well have heard much the same in the teaching of your faith." Matron looked at her, curiously, and nodded, almost in understanding. Such a belief as Vega's had some resonances in the life of Jesus, but those changed when they became part of an organized cultural experience and its monuments. She said nothing to Vega, who gathered her shopping bag and left for the city, to run a few errands and, of course, to stop at Café Pierre.

The last time or two, she had been the only European there. Today would be her last. Perhaps, those escaping the tedium of the Embassy would be there. And they were a small gathering of Embassy staff watching the literary jousting of Durrell and Pursewarden. The principals were interrupted from time to time by stones of wit thrown by the onlookers. Sitting a bit removed but still part of the group was Nessim, who moved his chair slightly as Vega entered so she could sit beside him. Pausing to consider Vega, Larry said: "You are a welcome respite from our all too frequent literary quibbles. But you have not erased them, for I have a few lines from a poem I hope to finish in a less uncertain time, a few lines brought on by a memory of you. Though not indiscreet, it is a bit presumptuous and poetic in that my view of you is based not on literal observation but on a poetic moment. Would you mind if I read it, in the presence of these louts, my apologies, to Nessim, as well as to you?" With less than polite interest, Vega said: "Please, do read it, a parting gesture. I leave in a few days." As would they all, they thought as did Durrell when he responded: "Though the occasion is regrettable, not unexpected but regrettable, let it be my parting gift, a poor thing but mine own:

The fixed star of the ancients was another Vega,
A candle burning high in the alps of heaven,
Shielded by rosy fingers on some sill
Above some darkly sifted lake. They also knew
This silence trying to perfect itself in words.

"Oh, I didn't intend to usher in silence. Quite the opposite."

Even Pursewarden was moved from his customary badinage: "Nonsense, Larry. You did the unforgivable. You introduced the real into the idle chatter of mere literati. Not nice. Now you make recompense. Miguel, another round on our friend here." While the drinks appeared and the assembled Embassy drudges looked askance at one another, Vega turned those deep blue and far seeing eyes on Larry and said: "How did you know?" He simply shook his head and picked up his glass and handed her the piece of paper from which he had read: "There are a few notes suggesting the rest of the poem. Someday, I'll find the finished poem, but not now, not in this place." Vega smiled, rose, and kissed him on the cheek: "Who knows where we will all be then. But then, as you once wrote: 'There is to write nicely, no human entity; it is merged in the All.'" She and Nessim left.

With no destination in mind, Vega and Nessim went toward the sea, drawn to it not as the border of Egypt where its lifeline, the Nile, led away from Africa and was joined, somewhat with all that lay on "the good side of the Med," but as the passageway to their own lives, to what they must do and be. Or at least that was certainly true for Nessim. If he were to live, he must do so on the other side of the Sea, for the Levant was closed to him and even the farm in Kenya was neither safe nor appealing for a man who could no longer be Nessim Hosnani. He could not imagine the anger that would be aroused by his departure with a new identity, hopefully untraceable. Memlik Pasha, venal though he was, was still a provincial potentate. Vega did not, though, think in these terms, only of the increasing desolation Nessim would face as he was drained by Memlik Pasha and sank steadily into social decline, so thinking she said: “How ever will you survive, not financially; for I am sure you will. But as a human being whose very life’s blood and family have been destroyed. Even your desert home is in ruins, the lands returning to the sand and salt marshes?” Nessim looked at her and said: “Let’s sit here for awhile.” And so they sat on a quiet, shaded bench on the Corniche and looked out at the old harbor which had lost the place it had in an earlier Egypt, second only to Rome, a place where love had died and power had lived. Perhaps little had changed. Turning to look at Vega, Nessim said: “With the failure of our attempt to secure a place for the Copts in the New Egypt, we became objects of derision and I a pariah to be plucked, as you implied. I know, of course, that many wait until I lack even a feather, but I will be gone before I am denuded. I will, perhaps, be among the first to see that Copts, and other Christians, will have no place safe and not even respectable in the New Egypt, nor in the state the Jews will found nor in Palestine nor in Syria, nor in the Levant in general. Exile, or to use a gentler term emigration, is our future. For those who remain, and some indomitable souls will remain, life will be a struggle. But a Coptic presence will continue but not with me.”

They looked out at the harbor where once an earlier Egypt had lost its identity to a younger and greater power, where love found it could not compete with anger and with Rome. They both knew that history can be churlish, indifferent to the individual and perhaps protective of the place with its spirit and local gods. But even they might be dormant for centuries, seen or felt only by the poet or by the illiterates who survived in obscurity. Turning to look at Nessim's downcast face, Vega said: "But surely you do not think you will be allowed to leave with any of your plumage intact. You will probably not be allowed to leave under any circumstances. For Memlik Pasha will need to parade you as a sign of his power, just as he flaunts your car and your wife in your face. Being stupid, ignorant, and venal, he needs your failure to assure himself of his importance. He is a little man with a big stick. And he will not let you go."

Nessim raised his head and looked over the harbor with its resonance of past loves and failures, its past redolent of exiles as well as conquerors and said: "There is a Prince of the Church who is willing for the poor to render unto God and let those with resources render unto Caesar, as long as the renderings pass through his priestly hands. He is a man with considerable power that will become absolute. For now and for me, he can be a force for good, for my good that is."

KOAN

SO HERE WE ARE AT LAST. THE WORD HORDE EMPTY

I had heard of rosy clouds when I was of earth but had seen them only in the kind of pictures found in children's books. Now I was walking on top of them, kicking up rosy bits of cloud, watching them fade quickly into the golden sunlight that seemed everywhere to put in profile bits of foliage and not, to my surprise, a card table with three men, two bearded and wearing tivennos (that's Greek for toga) and a clean shaven man in a fashionable black Italian cut suit. Even in this odd context I recognized them: Aristotle, Plato, and Frank Sinatra. They were playing cards, and Sinatra was obviously winning. He was all smiles. The two Greek philosophers failed to notice the cards he palmed.

"Sorry to bother you. But the man at the gate said I could only enter the clubhouse after I learned the meaning of life from you three, that you would tell me all, not bullshit me."

"Do be."

"Be do."

"Dobedobedo."

"That's it? Moronic rhymes."

"Not at all, chum. My songs and their dialogues and unreadable blather are merely diversions to occupy the pedants and the ignorant. You know, the serious ones who nod and say: 'Yes, yes, exactly.'"

"The ones who equate information with intelligence."

"Put them in a house with many libraries, leaving the real world open to those who can hear the laughter of the universe."

"So am I here to learn anything or just wonder what the clubhouse is like?"

"You might expect it to be like Athens of old, filled with the learned and the stupid. Actually, it's more like Vegas. No clocks."

"And what am I to learn from you?"

"Nothing. You've already looked past the shadows and seen the simple path. By the way, there is no clubhouse."

"Are there any women here or is this just an old boys club?"

"More women than men actually. Some have learned the way as we did through meditation and reflection and some were born to it and just paint their toenails, look at the world with its geniuses, and with a sly daughter of Sophia smile delivered sideways with a glance softly say the short version of The Serenity Prayer."